Sheila,
appreciate you
support

Gehenna

by H.M. Whitman

Happy
Reading!
H.M.
Whitman

RoseDog 🐾 Books
PITTSBURGH, PENNSYLVANIA 15238

RoseDog Books
585 Alpha Drive
Suite 103
Pittsburgh, PA 15238
Visit our website at www.rosedogbookstore.com

ISBN: 978-1-6442-6814-8
eISBN: 978-1-6442-6791-2

EZRA ISLAND

My name is Celeste. It is the beginning of summer. Long days at the beach, boat rides, food on the grill, and sunshine! That's my definition of summer. Today is going to be a good day, I am heading to the beach with some friends. The plan is to head to Ezra Island which is a good half hour boat ride. We like to bring a cooler with food, drinks and sometimes a tent to do some beach camping!

Which is exactly what we plan on doing this time. The Island is so big we have never explored the whole thing, and the water around the island is very deep which makes it nice, we are able to bring the boat close to shore to anchor it.

The group consists of myself, my cousin Sophie who happens to be just two years older than me, Sophie's husband Jackson, and my dearest friends Isaac and Kora. The "Fab Five", a nickname that derives from nothing, we gave it to ourselves. The day is unusually hot, the temperature gage in the jeep reads eighty six. That is about ten degrees hotter than average this time of year. I am in route to pick up Kora who lives in a cute little bungalow style house near the beach.

The town we live in sits on a beautiful section of Lake Superior, which is the largest of the great lakes, and possibly the coldest. The average water temperature at the beginning of summer is around forty degrees and by summer's end is still only around sixty degrees, if we are lucky! But that never deters us from enjoying it. The huge sand dunes surrounding much of the shoreline are visible from almost anywhere in our small town, climbing like giants toward the sky and changing slightly in shape when the strong winds blow.

There is more water in Lake Superior than the rest of the great lakes combined, which makes it like a fresh water ocean and at the same time makes one realize how they need to respect its power and size.

But what I find most incredible is that there are over four hundred islands spread around this great body of water, Ezra being one of them, and it sits straight out from our marina.

Kora and I are thirty two years old. We have no children and no husbands. We did not intend for this to be the case. We both had dreamed of our weddings, sat and talked for hours about the kind of man we would spend the rest of our lives with. Talked about the children we would have, how many and what their names would be. So many of the dreams we had growing up have not come to pass.

As I gaze down the side streets I pass, the water is visible from every one. I drive down Potter Street toward Kora's house and find her sitting on her front steps smoking a cigarette. Her black curly hair is sitting in a messy bun on top of her head and she is wearing the white sundress I gave her.

There are large peach colored flowers on it and I think it looks so much better on her against her dark skin than it did on me with my ivory complexion and auburn hair. I ended up buying another one of the same dress for myself in a pastel green. She smiles big when she notices me. It seems she is looking forward to the day as well. Kora jumps up, runs to my vehicle, throws her bag in the back seat, jumps in, plugs her phone in and searches for one of her favorite tunes. The voice of Rupert Holmes begins singing the song 'Escape' on the radio. We both laugh. I turn it up and we continue the drive to the marina.

Sophie, Jackson and Isaac are already there sitting on the boat. Jackson's boat is amazing! It is an old pontoon boat, but like on steroids. Perfect for playing around in the bay and taking over to the Island. It has a huge motor on it and there is so much room to sit or just lay around on. Plus, there is a deck on top. Jackson bought a detachable slide that hooks onto the upper deck which is a blast out in the water. Even though the boat is super old, it is Jackson's baby and he takes really good care of it. It truly is the best boat ever.

Jackson takes care of everything he owns. Including himself. He works out and eats healthy. He has olive colored skin, big brown eyes and a receding hairline so he keeps it shaved quite short.

He has a stocky build he inherited from his father he claims, and gets mad at the fact that Isaac who is taller and naturally wiry can eat anything, does not work out and never gains a pound. Isaac has these big blue eyes that are so welcoming. Probably the kindest soul I have ever met. My cousin Sophie and I look nothing alike. She looks like her father's family. Dirty blonde hair and hazel eyes and a bit of a shorter stature at five feet three inches.

Isaac turns our way as we pull into a parking spot. He raises his beer in our direction. I get out, skip around the side and pop open the back end to grab the cooler and bag. Jackson and Isaac begin walking down the dock toward us. "New plan!" Isaac yells before reaching us.

"Great." Kora mumbles.

"We have decided that it is time to go exploring. To take a walk and see what there is to see and what wonders lie within the woods of Ezra Island."

"You know what wonders lie within dear Isaac. We have discussed this before. More than once actually." I say.

"Wonder who will miss you when you are gone." Kora questions. Isaac laughs.

"Seriously. " He says. "This time is going to be the last time we have a chance to have this kind of adventure. All of us, without any additions."

"What are you talking about Isaac?" I ask.

"You know what I mean. We are all getting older. That means weddings and children and serious life shit. I'm surprised it hasn't happened already, to all of us," He explains and looks at Jackson. "Besides, we all have an entire week off of work! It is the perfect time."

Kora and I exchange looks that I suppose could be taken as a look of conceding to the idea, which I suppose we did without saying so. Besides, I think we all realize that we have discussed doing exactly what Isaac is suggesting too many times for us to ignore it. Isaac and Jackson head to the marina store to grab some more supplies.

The boat ride to the island is perfect. The water is calm, the sun is hot and the drinks are cold. We talk about the idea of exploring the island with some hesitation. But, none of us can deny the feeling we have. It feels like something is pulling us to do this, and has for a very long time now. Isaac shares that he has had the nagging feeling worse than ever before and that is why he brought it up as soon as he hooked up with Jackson and Sophie that morning. As we near the island it is a fore sure thing, we will hike around and see what happens. Worst case scenario, we disappear forever.

Arriving at our usual spot, we anchor the boat and everyone grabs what they can to haul to shore. After a couple of trips back to the boat, everything we brought has been relocated to the beach. It takes a bit of time to organize and load our backpacks for the adventure. As soon as we are done doing that we decide that we want to head out right away. "Let the fun begin." Isaac says. And with that we are off.

We walk for a few miles and are already feeling the need for a break. The sun is beating down on us through the camouflage of trees and it is very hot. Just as I am feeling like we really need to find some sort of cover that could protect us from the heat for a while, Jackson notices a fast running stream up ahead. It looks way too inviting to pass up. Everyone takes off running toward it, I am the first one to throw my shoes off and jump in. The water feels amazing! I turn over and float on my back allowing myself to drift downstream. As I look up toward the sky I admire the billowy clouds that can be transformed into all kinds of different images. Then, I look to my right and notice a cute little frog sitting on the embankment. I lower my foot in the shallow stream to slow myself because for some reason I have the urge to grab this frog. Success! I manage to get a hold of it but I am surprised with how slippery he feels. I scream, and without so much as a thought, I throw the frog, straight up in the air.

Kora, who is floating behind me, screams as she notices the frog falling straight down toward her head! She quickly raises her hands above her head to try and catch the frog, but misses. It lands on her chest which makes her squeal again. She proceeds to grab the frog and throw the poor thing back into the air, yelling about how slimy he is. I am laughing so hard. As the frog comes down, once again, I cup my hands, to not give it a chance to land. I carefully redirect it toward Sophie this time. Isaac decides he needs to intervene on the frog's behalf. He steps in front of Sophie and catches the poor thing in mid-flight and sets it back into the water. We watch the frog as it swims away, looking as though he has had one too many lemon drop shots or something, which makes all of us burst out with laughter.

We leave the stream and hike for a couple more hours, then decide to make camp before it gets dark. It is really nice to sit around the fire, visit and catch up. Each one of us are so busy in our daily lives, it makes it difficult to coordinate everyone's schedule so that we can all get together anymore. The conversation is filled with stories about things that some of us are aware of and others are not. The talk continues until everyone is so tired it is difficult to find the next word so we head to our tents.

As I crawl into my sleeping bag there is a brief feeling of peacefulness that sweeps over me. I feel quite blessed, no matter how many bad things have happened to me, there are also so many good things going on in my life.

I realize this and yet still have that same, something is missing feeling inside that is with me always. I try very hard to not let it control my every moment. I am able to feel happiness and have fun times but the sadness is there as well.

Morning came quickly but everyone's mood is still positive. We make breakfast over the campfire and sit around for a while drinking coffee. Packing up our gear goes swiftly and we are ready to head out. On this day, Isaac leads and the rest of us follow.

As time ticks by on day two, our positive mood begins to diminish some. We have not come across any kind of sign that there is anything otherworldly lurking on the island and discuss the fact that we may not find anything. We also discuss the fact that we are all crazy because, NOT finding the slides that could possibly erase us from this world would be what is disappointing!

One thing we do come across is a huge apple tree. Sitting down, enjoying the apples provides a nice reprieve from the continual look and listen thing we are doing and they are delicious. As night approaches, we choose a spot to set up camp a little less enthusiastically. I think we are all drained from walking, I couldn't begin to guess how many miles, in the hot sun that is depleting all of the water and energy from our bodies as fast as we can replace it.

I can't help but wonder if this was a good idea. We could have been camping right on the beach these last two days. Sunshine, shade as needed, swimming, eating and drinking. As my mind drifts further into scenarios that could have been I feel myself drifting off to sleep.

On the morning of the third day we decide to hit the trail hard and take less breaks. We have barely began hiking when we see this oh so inviting waterfall. Instead of killing the plan all together, we agreed to stop and play but then walk later into the day. Isaac and Kora decide they are going to climb along the edge of the fall and jump in. I lie down in the shallow water and close my eyes. I am reaching a state of being completely relaxed when water splashing in my face startles me. I sit up and see Jackson and Isaac wrestling in the water in front of me. Sophie jumps on Jackson's back and takes him under with her. Then Isaac begins walking toward me with a smirky grin on his face. Before I have a chance to move he has me by the feet and is dragging me into deeper water. I begin kicking and screaming, trying to break free to no avail. Finally I stop and succumb to being submerged in the cool water.

We probably played longer than planned but we are back hiking. The trail we are on, if you can call it that, is littered with tree roots sticking up out of the ground and a clay like base. The Island has never been inhabited as far as I know so it is free of any kind of man made development to make this even a little easier.

Most parts of the island is heavily wooded but there are also parts you stumble into displaying a beautiful opening releasing you from the grip of the thickset trees.

"I'm hungry." Sophie yells. "Let's stop and eat here." As we get food out it is obvious we are getting low on our supply.

"After tonight we should consider heading back toward the boat." Jackson suggests. Nobody responds, but we know he is right.

By the end of the third day, we had walked what seemed like forever through the woods looking for the slides. Losing faith in the legend on more than one occasion, yet still continuing on with the escapade. Two overnights and three full days of walking in search of them. Stopping for some R and R every now and then, including a bit of fun.

And now, here they are. We can see them. All of us can see them! The feeling is overwhelming, almost unbearable, for us all. They are huge! The stairs, the only part of them that can be seen on each one, ascend into the clouds. They stand together enveloped with the surrounding wood acting like a cloak. I walk slowly to the center of the four ginormous sets of stairs. The four separate sets of stairs are positioned in a circular fashion with enough room in the middle for the others to join me so that we can all stand together in awe.

After a long period of silence from everyone, all standing in a state of disbelief from what we were witnessing, Kora finally says. "It's real. It is really real you guys."

"Now to decide…..which slide to take." That was the decision that was made during these last couple of days. If the legend was real and we were presented with entrance to another realm, that we should take that as a sign and the five of us be willing to go on that journey, no matter the cost or what it will entail. Each of us have reason to believe in something greater than the suffering we have all endured in this place that we call home. Maybe that's what has connected us all these years, a common bond of souls that have experienced much. All of us feeling the emptiness inside, the relentless nagging that makes us believe something is missing, and the search to find out what it is.

The conversation between us is gripped with a nervousness. Isaac believes we should each take our own slide and see each other at some point 'On the other side.' I remind Isaac that there are four slides and five of us. Kora wants us all to go up the same one. Sophie & Jackson know they will be staying together and make that very clear to all of us. We all comment how it would be nice to know which slide is which season. Apparently, each of us believing in the part of the myth that says each slide represents a season. And no one wants to end up in a frozen tundra dressed as we are. Summer wear!

We are all sitting on the ground staring up into the sky. Everyone looking at the stairs on the slides disappearing into the clouds. Everyone except Isaac. He is pacing.

"I think we should just camp here tonight. Build a fire and stay one more night before doing this. It will give us more time to figure out what we want to do, IF we still want to do this." He said. After a short pause, I agree, and then so did the rest of the group.

We work quickly to get our tents set up. Sophie thought it would be a good idea to set them up outside of the peculiar looking entrance to 'Gehenna.' Gehenna is what everyone calls whatever lies at the bottom of the slides, the name which has been around as long as anyone can remember. "Well just think guys, it has to be pretty amazing there or so many wouldn't be trying to go. Never to return home!" Jackson burst out with a nervous laugh.

"I like your logic Jackson. Not so sure they are choosing to stay though." Isaac pipes in. The entire group is tired and nervous. One at a time we go to our tents to get some sleep. Jackson & Sophie are first. Then me, Kora, and last but not least Isaac crawls into his very small one man tent. Kora wants to talk.

"What should we do? Do you want to go up the same one? I hope I don't end up in the winter season. How do we even know this is real?" Kora asks.

"Is what real?" I ask.

"The seasons." She says. "How do we know that's what each slide represents?" But at the end of her question her voice fades off quietly. Jackson filled Isaac, Kora and me in on this myth not long after we arrived in Paradise. Paradise is the name of the town we live in, and it can be very much like paradise.

There are some people in and around our community who claim to be mediums. These people allege to have received information from the deceased who have went to Gehenna. That is where many of the stories and information comes from. These same people warn that some of the information they get is through pictures the dead show them. They say to remember that the meaning could get skewed in the way they interpret the pictures.

Knowing this, people in the town of Paradise, and rumor has it in other places too, know the stories well. It is rumored that people in other towns, cities, even other countries have these same things happening to them, slides appearing and having missing loved ones. The town of Paradise know the many people who have been lost in the woods of Ezra Island, or as some believe, to the waters of Lake Superior. They have been told the stories since they have been old enough to listen and understand. From the time they were able to leave their mother's side they have been warned about the Island.

And the more parents warned, the more curious the children would become. As the children grow and get older they want to see if they can find these elusive slides. Maybe they would appear for them. For us. Maybe these missing people were living on the Island somewhere and just didn't want to come back. As one gets older yet, they realize that all of these people did not all want to leave and live on an Island. Besides, someone would have seen something at some point. Or, one of the lost would have returned. Neither has happened. There is also the fact that many have searched this island and found nothing, helping lend to the belief that the great lake had swallowed yet another loved one.

There is another part to the myth that intrigues some. It causes some to look for these slides with great intensity, to hope they will appear for them. To actually climb them and slide down into....well no one knows where for sure. This part says that you enter a land that clones our world. Except for one thing. It is where some of our loved ones are. The ones we have lost to death. That the island has the porthole to get to them again. It is where they go to be redeemed before entering the next realm. But it is not all loved ones. The person you lost has to have done something to move into this cloned world. They had to be an immoral, sinful person here. Committing the worst transgressions against divine law known to man. The one you seek to save has done horrific things. Something that will not be forgiven without redemption.

Legend says they end up in the season they hated most, adding to their suffering and sharing their land with other lost souls and otherworldly creatures. If when you slide down, you do not end up in the season your loved one resides then your journey to find them will be that much harder. The seasons in this parallel universe are separate but not disconnected. It goes on to say that they leave our world and go to this parallel universe but if you can find your loved one and help them to understand the effect their sin had, to ask for forgiveness and want it, then they will be able to move on, to the final realm, where our tears will be dried and there will be no more pain or suffering. Or, they will be forever stuck in this land, feeling the pain and guilt and any other unsettled emotion from their sins forever. Their own Hell.

The wind is blowing softly, the smell of wild ginger looms in the air and the sun has finally turned the temperature down. I lay my head on my small camping pillow and let my mind begin to drift...

The Cabin & The Shack

It was fall. The air was crisp. The smells of fresh cut grass, autumn leaves, and smoke from a freshly lit fireplace surrounded me.

I have come to this cabin many times with my family. It was probably a four hour drive from our home. Thinking back to the last time I visited the family cabin is a kind of torture I force upon myself. There is nothing I can do to rid myself of the memory, so when it continues encompassing my brain and starts to become too overwhelming to deal with, my solution is to go back to that day-and relive the event that haunts me.

I will pick a time when I am not out in public, not at work, not in a place that requires any kind of presence on my part and allow myself to feel the raw emotions from fifteen years ago and bring them back into my present. It seems as though I must do this every so often in order to keep my sanity as odd as that may sound.

Fifteen years ago I was living at home with my parents. The memory starts with me sitting at the Island in our kitchen eating a bagel. My grandfather called to ask if anyone had plans to use the cabin for the upcoming weekend. Grandpa and his buddy Arnie were planning a hunting weekend. He spoke with my father and I recall my parents discussing whether we were going to be using the cabin that weekend or not. They concluded that we would not, not by accident I am sure, therefore Grandpa and Arnie would get their last hunt of the season in.

As the end of the week neared, my Mother began to make plans for a weekend getaway of our own. One that sounded God awful, involving lots of traffic, crowded malls and an overabundance of chain restaurants. I did what was necessary to be excluded from the upcoming festivities of fun.

"I would like to go to the cabin with Grandpa." I exclaimed. My mother and father exchanged looks. Initially it was a look of I think not, then the re- alization that there was an opportunity for them to have a weekend alone be- came apparent.

"Oh and Sarah asked me if I could spend Friday night with her, her family is leaving Saturday for their vacation doing a color tour of Northern Michigan. They plan on driving to the Keweenaw Peninsula and camping each night in a new colorful destination. Her parents say it is the best colors around this time of year."

"Celeste, you are rambling." My father said. "That is fine if you want to stay at Sarah's on Friday as long as you are up and on the road early to get to the cabin before dark. That would mean you need to be to the cabin no later than six o'clock that night. You should see if your cousin Sophie wants to go with."

"Oh and give your Grandfather a call right now so he knows to expect you for Saturday." My mother chimed in. "I think Sophie is going to be visiting her mother this weekend."

"You mean your sister?" I said

"Yes, Celeste." My mother inhaled deeply. "My sister, her mother."

I agreed to all of their conditions. As I was leaving the kitchen I tried to hide the huge smile on my face.

Knowing I didn't have to suffer through driving with my parents for hours, being able to stay at Sarah's for one night and one at the cabin with grandpa and Arnie. I loved my grandfather, idolized him actually. There had been so many fun times, just the two of us.

Grandpa liked to take me fishing, hunting, and tell me stories about when he was young, some of which were quite exaggerated, I hope! One of his favorites was of him and his older brother stealing chickens from a farm down the road. Grandpa loved telling that one. In his words he claimed that family had more chickens than they needed anyway. The excitement of getting into the chicken coop, past the barking dogs, past the cows and horses, who were all stirred up because of the unexpected company in the late evening hours, was almost more rewarding than seeing the look on his mother's face when they came through the front door with food for the family.

This grandfather was my mother's father. According to my mother, grandpa grew up very poor. There was always a shortage of food to feed everyone. Always a shortage of pretty much everything one needs to survive. A family with thirteen children and no father. Well, there was a father until my grandfather who was somewhere in the middle of the thirteen , number seven I believe, was about twelve years old.

At the age of twelve, his father, my great grandfather went into an old work shed behind the barn and hung himself from the rafters.

That is one story my grandfather never talked about. When I would ask, he would tell me that he wasn't interested in sharing anything about that. There was no sense in pushing the subject, not with him anyway. I tried to get more details from my mother on the subject, but didn't get anywhere with her either.

I ran upstairs to my bedroom to start packing. It was that time of year that you just weren't sure if you needed a long sleeve t-shirt or a snow suit. I decided to pack so that I could layer. I also planned on bringing warmer clothes just in case I ended up doing some hunting myself at the cabin. At the time of year it was, the hunt would have been for partridge. A very small bird once it was dressed out, but pretty tasty when prepared correctly.

As for grandpa and his enjoyment of hunting, I believe, was precisely that, enjoyment of the hunt. Sure, he enjoyed wild game, the taste, but the reward for him was probably the same as it was back when he was twelve years old- getting a hold of a chicken without being caught so that he could help feed his brothers and sisters. The bird, deer or bear was just icing on the cake. In fact, grandpa gave lots of the wild game he hunted and killed away to needy families in the area.

That day was pretty uneventful. I did call Sophie at some point but she was going to visit her mother in the hospital on Saturday, so she reluctantly declined my invite to go along. Sophie's mother, my aunt, was what you would call 'sick in the head.' She was in and out of hospitals since I could remember.

Later that evening I went back to my room to finish packing. I started to yawn as I put the last of what I was bringing into my weekender. I hadn't realized how late it was. My bed looked really inviting, so I undressed and threw just a tank on, my favorite form of sleeping apparel and crawled into bed.

I remember when I woke the next morning my bedroom was filled with light. There was no school that day so I hadn't set my alarm. It was nine o clock. I couldn't believe how long I had slept. Must have been the fact that I went to bed so late. Which certainly wasn't the first time. Sarah and I used to have sleepovers where we would do a movie fest, we would try and stay up all night. It never happened, not once, but we never gave up on the idea.

"Celeste, are you up?" I hear my mother yelling from the bottom of the stairs. "Your father is making pancakes. You need to come and eat, we are going to be leaving soon.

"Did you call your grandfather? Is he ok with you staying Saturday?" So many questions I remember thinking, my brain isn't fully awake yet.

"I will be right down." I yelled. I forgot to call grandpa, I will on my way to Sarah's I thought. Besides, he wouldn't care if I came to spend a night. I would tell them I got the A ok so nobody worried. They could take off to enjoy their weekend of shopping and eating without any concern for me.

When I entered the kitchen I could see that there were enough pancakes for ten people, I shook my head slightly thinking how different things were for us compared to grandpa growing up with never enough food. There was some small talk about our weekend plans and my parent's expectations for me with mine. I scarfed down the last couple bites of pancakes and put my plate in the dishwasher, ran up to my room, grabbed a quick shower and I was off.

I always loved the drive to Sarah's house. It went down this back country road, filled with winding turns and roller coaster type hills. Her driveway was really long, with a couple of winding turns as well. She was outside when I pulled up that morning feeding her horse. The field that the horse was in wasn't very far from the house so I saw her right away. "We should take a ride later." She yelled as I got out of my car.

"Sure." I said. I didn't enjoy riding like she did, but I didn't hate it either. That day is a bit of a blur, I remember things we did but don't recall the conversation, what we had for dinner, or even what movie we watched before crashing for the night. The memories I have from the time I left her house are quite vivid though. I even recall the song playing when I first got in the car to leave. Garth Brooks was singing 'The Dance.' I used to love that song.

The drive to the cabin went by slow, maybe because I was by myself. I still hadn't called to let my grandfather know I was coming and now I couldn't, the cell signal heading to the cabin was pretty much a complete dead zone. There were some areas where you could get a signal but it was hit and miss. I figured it didn't matter anyway. When I got there, grandpa and Arnie would probably be sitting in the cabin, cleaning their guns, talking of the day, or cleaning the birds they had killed on the day's hunt.

As I round the final turn before having to veer sharp left to get to the cabin road, there was a flock of snowbirds right in the middle of the road. They all flew at the same time, in the same direction, when they felt the vibration of my car on the road I suppose. I thought about how cool that looked.

Once on the dirt road I slow down, the road is not the greatest, full of tree stumps sticking up and big holes that hadn't been tended to in way too long. The cabin has had lots of use, but nobody ever bothered to make sure the road leading in was adequate.

It wasn't dark yet but just about. The last glimpse of the sun was setting, making the cabin look almost spooky. I don't recall ever feeling that way, but that night, as the old, well maintained structure came into view, I felt reluctant. Why in the world would I, I wondered. The strangest, most uncomfortable feeling came over me.

It was fall. The air was crisp. The smells of fresh cut grass, autumn leaves, and smoke from a freshly lit fireplace surrounded me. I have come to this cabin many times with my family. There was a light on that I could see was in the living room area. No other lights were on though. The small shed off to the side had a light on as well. I thought maybe grandpa and Arnie were cleaning the birds in the shed, or putting the four wheelers away.

The place where we parked wasn't any better than the road coming in. A person would pretty much just pick a spot in an area that had been cleared for parking off to the right a little ways from the cabin itself. When I got out of the car, I didn't bother grabbing my bag.

I figured I would first let my presence be known and retrieve it later. My first step was right into a cold puddle of water. "Damn it" I said under my breath. My walk to the shed was more careful, watching the uneven ground as I went. Once at the shed door, I could see that there was no one inside, including the four wheelers. Where could they be? Grandpa only stayed out hunting during the day light, at least has for quite some time now as he has gotten older.

When I opened the cabin door I yelled but no one answered. There was a fire going, a few dirty dishes in the sink and two coffee mugs sitting on the homemade dining room table. The fire was burning hot so it must have been filled not that long ago. Why would they leave and go back out again? Then it hit me, I bet something happened to one of the four wheelers. They must have come back for some tools to fix it and headed back out. I decided to just sit by the fire and wait for them. I sunk into the chair, allowed my eyes to shut and began to relax.

Moments later, I thought I heard something outside. It sounded like screaming. I tried to lift my head up from the side of the oversized chair I was sitting on. I think I had started to fall asleep. Still groggy, I pulled myself back up to a sitting position. There it was again, yelling, a man. It was getting closer.

I jumped up and ran to a window to look out. It was so dark outside... I couldn't see a thing. I peered into the darkness trying to focus my eyes so they could adjust. It wasn't working though, the moon wasn't even visible to cast a shadow of light. Then, THUD! Something had ran into the outside wall of the cabin! I remember how loud it was. I jumped and fell backwards onto the floor. My heart felt like it was going to pound right out of my chest. I scooted myself back from the window while still on the floor. BAM! The front door flung open! My head reeled around to see what had just burst in.

There was a man, standing there. A huge man covered in blood. His face was so bloody I couldn't tell what he looked like, his breathing was so heavy his chest was rising and falling with great force. It was apparent that he was in great distress. The bloodied man stood there for a few seconds staring back at me. "Please help me." It was so faint I could barely hear him. "Please, I just need the keys to a vehicle or a phone, please", he said again, a little louder this time. He turned and looked behind him and then back at me. "HELP ME!"

I was frozen. I don't think my eyes had blinked since the door was thrown open. Then Arnie was there, behind the man, and grandpa behind Arnie. Arnie had his hand raised up above his head, there was something in it. It looked like a piece of wood and he slammed it right into the back of this man's head.

And with that, the man fell to the cabin floor. My eyes looked up... and met with Grandpa's.

Arnie grabbed the man by his feet and drug him into the cabin. Grandpa still looking at me helped Arnie pick this man up and set him into a chair. Out came the duct tape, over the mouth then around the entire body. Nobody had said a word yet. A bit of time went by and then, "The final hunt of the year is different from any other hunt Celeste." Arnie is going to explain this to me? I don't want his explanation. What is going on!

"Your grandfather and I came to discover a long time ago there is a hunt more thrilling and enjoyable than any other. We always save the final hunt for this. Hunting man is something nobody wants to talk about. It's quite exhilarating actually. When we hunt an animal, we are the alpha male, superior in our thinking and with the weaponry we use to kill. To hunt something that is an equal, in the sense that our brain capacity is fairly balanced, our bodies function in the same manner, and we understand the meaning of life and death. Some believe the meaning of life is to find your gift and the purpose of life is to give it away. Other's think it is about conquering and constantly moving up in the world, proving your worth. I, on the other hand, believe simply that people are not necessarily looking for the meaning of life as much as they are looking for lots of experiences that make them feel alive.

And, man fully understands that life ends. So because man understands these things he values life, and the hunt turns into a frenzied hysteria, with uncontrolled emotions igniting from the hunter and from the hunted." Arnie sat himself down in front of the man that is taped to the chair.

"The hunt sir, will start tomorrow. We always do a pre hunt, just to get everyone warmed up. The real hunt begins in the morning, usually coming to an end by dusk. You will be fed shortly and then laid into a comfortable bed to get some rest. We want this to be a fair hunt, you need to have your strength and wits about you." The man never took his eyes off of the floor. He gave Arnie a slight nod to let him know he understood. Grandpa walked past me heading into the small kitchen area. He stopped at my side and spoke softly.

"I wish you would have called, I wish you would have never seen this. There are things people do in their lives that belong only to them. This here, what you are witnessing, is mine. One day, you will have something that is only yours, something you will not share with anyone else. I am sorry I have to say this to you... do not share this thing of mine with anyone Celeste. Ever. We will never speak of this. You have learned of this by accident but do not let it affect who I am to you. This has nothing to do with you and me, and it never will. Do whatever it is you need to and make this a bad dream, a non-memory. When morning comes, move on. Make this night a chapter in the past. But don't close the book Celeste, just turn the page." And with that he continued into the kitchen.

I didn't know what to do. I know I was in a state of shock. I couldn't let this poor man die. Be hunted like an animal, what kind of maniacs were Arnie and grandpa. My thoughts were spinning, trying to figure out how to help him. I was still on the floor with my back perched against the wall. The man was facing away from me. I put my head down on my knees. I couldn't think straight, this was all too unreal.

The smell of bacon was overwhelming, I could hear it sizzling, I heard pots clanging, doors opening and shutting. Sitting in the same spot on the floor for what must have been thirty minutes without budging an inch I finally pulled myself up to my feet. My legs were unsteady and my eyes burned. I looked at the back of the man's head and noticed his hair was matted to one spot where the blood was drying. I begin to move, walking past the kitchen area and into one of the bunk rooms, I climbed to the top bunk and let my body crash to the mattress. I didn't want to look at Arnie or grandpa. My first thought was that I need to leave and never come back to this place again. That poor man, he looked so scared. Maybe he will be able to escape with his life. Maybe I should free him.

If I do, that means he would go to the police, tell them about this place and what happened.

They would come and arrest my grandpa. Arnie and Grandpa would go to prison for this. They should go to prison for this! How many times had they done this kind of hunt here? I heard Arnie's voice telling me that if I was hungry there was lots to eat. I was starving before the hunted man ran into the cabin, but now, I just felt frazzled, confused and extremely tired. How on earth could I sleep, how could I stay in this place, but it was a tired like nothing I had ever felt. Finally, as if I didn't have a choice, I found myself succumbing to my heavy eyelids and allowing them to close.

When I woke I had no idea what time it was. The room was well lit with daylight. My mind started to race. Instantly, I was back in the moment with the hunter and everything that had been said and done the night before. It was running through my mind over and over and over again until I put my hands up to my head, a hand on each ear and started to squeeze as hard as I could. Maybe this will make it stop, I wanted it to go away! This was not something I could deal with, I didn't want to deal with this craziness! The room starting spinning and I felt dizzy and weak. I wanted to run out but couldn't find my feet or the floor beneath them. Everything stopped. I climbed down to the bottom bunk, leaned over the trash can next to the bed and started throwing up.

While I was bent over getting sick, I could hear the familiar creaking sound of the bedroom door when it was being opened. I didn't look to see who it was, instead I continued to dry heave and when it finally stopped I still would not turn around to see who entered the room. I wasn't even sure if anyone was still there. I gathered enough strength to walk over to the window and look out. My grandpa was walking across the dirt drive with the stranger at his side. The stranger was tied up with what looked like binder twine. My heart was in my throat and pounding so hard that I'm sure if I had looked down I would have been able to see it beating through my shirt. So there it was, the end of life as I knew it, my life will never be the same. No matter what I do, this was going to forever haunt me.

I stared out the window and watched Arnie walk from the house on the same route Grandpa took with the stranger to the barn. He stopped outside of the barn door looking inside. I could see that he was speaking to someone in the barn. I assumed who that was. My head slid down to rest on the window-ledge and my eyes focused on the open door that Arnie was facing. It must have been cold outside because I could see Arnie's breath, it exited his mouth in a white smoky mist. There was another white smoky mist coming from inside, I couldn't see who it belonged to. They were hidden just far enough out of view. I can remember the mist that was coming from inside the barn exiting so quickly it was forming a cloud, piling up and flowing with the wind upward and then off to the side, then over Arnie's head.

Arnie turned away from the barn and walked over to the fence off to the side. He put a foot up on the bottom rail and leaned against it. My eyes were so focused on Arnie I hadn't noticed my grandfather leaving the barn until he joined his friend at the fence. After a short bit, both Arnie and Grandpa walked back into the barn. What happened next was beyond belief. The stranger darted out of the barn, he was no longer tied at the wrists, and was running for his life. He was heading straight for the woods beyond the cabin, the woods that you could be lost for days in. Endless acres of hardwood, swamp and small lakes. I watched as about ten minutes later grandpa and Arnie very calmly left out of the barn on their four wheelers, driving in the same direction the stranger had ran. This isn't happening I kept telling myself.

I went to grab my bag, then remembered I hadn't brought it in. Walking out to my car left a knot in my stomach, I had a nervousness just stepping outside. The nausea was so strong I had to stop for a moment and breathe, not sure whether I was going to be sick again or not.

Finally, at my car I regained some composure, opened the driver door, got in and locked all the doors. I remember thinking I don't know what to do but I have to get out of here! I tried to start the car but it wouldn't start....then... everything went black.

I was outside. Somehow I was outside…in the woods. I wondered how long had I been lying there and also wondered where I was. My head was throbbing, I must have been hit hard. I sat up and looked around but nothing looked familiar. Then… a strange noise. It didn't sound like it was far from where I was laying. It scared me instantly. I was so anxious already and now just wanted to get as far away from that noise as possible. Maybe that noise is what was responsible for my head hurting, for me no longer being in my car but wherever I am now. I needed be quiet. Should I crawl? Maybe I should just stay very still behind this tree. I could run. And then I heard the noise again. It sounded like the crunching of leaves. Suddenly, the trees were a blur. I was running. I didn't want to look behind me so I continued to run without stopping. I don't know for how long but my legs started to cramp. I began to slow my pace until it became more of a walk, then stopped completely and leaned on a tree for support to catch my breath, still continuing to look behind me to make sure nothing was or had followed.

Scanning the area I could see something not too far in the distance. It looked like a structure of some sort. After a few minutes of being still and listening I moved closer until I got a better view. It appeared to be a large clock tower. A clock tower in the middle of the woods, how strange I thought. I leaned up against another tree for a bit longer than started moving towards the large structure. As I approached I could see other buildings. There was even a street, sidewalks, street lights. No people. Before I had an opportunity to check things out better, I noticed that there was a man down the street a ways. I could not get a good look at him but it looked as though he was middle aged, wearing a dark suit and was quite slender.

The man was unusually tall. As he got closer, I could see that he had a sinister smile on his face. I avoided heading toward him. I looked around and noticed rows of perfectly lined trees just across the way. I began walking toward them. As I glanced behind me one more time to see what the man was doing, he was closer yet. Only across the street now, still smiling. I began to walk into the perfect rows of trees and would not turn around.

After a few minutes I could hear the sound of waves crashing onto a shore. Then a beautiful beach came into view. The water was glistening in the sun.

The color is what I would describe as unclouded or clear and I could see every rock, every ripple of sand, anything lying beneath the water was so obvious.

The wind was blowing softly and there was nothing but sandy beach as far as the eye could see. Clear turquoise colored water and white sand. It was stunning, and warm! Even though it was fall it felt more like July. I began to feel like I was in some sort of Twilight Zone. I took a step and then remembered the tall man. It made me turn in all directions and look for him. He was nowhere to be seen. The sun felt so nice and I was feeling so exhausted. I decided to walk a bit further down the beach until I came across an area of large rocks. I climbed up on one, looked around again to make sure the man had not followed me and then lied down. The waves were rolling up to the bottom of the rock I was on. It was so peaceful for the moment, I involuntarily drifted off to sleep.

Suddenly, I was startled by a loud screeching noise. I sat up so fast I almost fell off the rock. What on earth is that noise! Then I could see it, some sort of prehistoric looking bird. Not sure what it was but it was a ways down the beach. Maybe a sandhill crane I thought. I sat there for a moment then jumped off the rock. The sun was still warm but I could tell it was getting to be later in the day. The wind had picked up as well. As I started to walk down the beach I realized I was not sure where I was going, didn't know where I was but knew that I had to find a way out. The only thing I could see was water and sand. Hopefully something else would come into view at some point.

After walking for what felt like an hour I saw something in the distance. It looked like a massive wall of green. I couldn't be sure what it was. I continued walking and as I got closer I could see it clearly, it was an island. There was no way around it. I noticed the distance through the water to the land on the other side was not far but there seemed to be quite a current circulating around it. So, here were my options. I swim to the Island, hoping I don't get caught and stuck in the current, floating around the Island in circles with no escape until I perish. Dramatic. Probably. My other option would be to turn back around and walk in the opposite direction for who knows how long to come across who knows what if anything. A swim to the Island won out. After all, I was a strong swimmer, I thought. I put my foot in the water to check the temperature and it felt warm. That was good. I jumped in and started to swim. The water was deep... well over my head anyway. I was immediately swept into the current, the feeling of not being in control scared me and I panicked a little. I was able to calm myself and swam with it. Slowly but surely making progress toward the land. I managed to grab a branch from a tree that was leaning into my path, almost losing my grip when I first grabbed hold. I pulled and held on as hard as I could and made it onto the dirt embankment.

I sat down on the top of the embankment I had just climbed up.

As I focused my eyes back across the water and onto the beach I saw something...someone. It appeared to be a man, and he was headed my way. It wasn't the unusually tall man. This man looked huge and appeared to have something behind him. My heart was in my throat. I was frozen. I tried to move my legs to help me stand but they were shaking so badly I struggled. My eyes were straining trying to see what was behind his back. It appeared to be black in color and came up over his shoulders which I hadn't noticed at first. As I was backing away from the embankment, I pulled my eyes away from the man and turned toward the woods. It was quite thick. I didn't want to stay on a straight path from where I started so I zig zagged at a fast pace through the trees. When I looked back... I no longer saw the man.

I proceeded with a fast paced walk continuing to zig zag through the large trees. After what felt like another 30 minutes of walking I noticed something up ahead. A structure of some sort. As I got closer I could see that I had come across, an old, abandoned shack. I approached with caution trying to keep myself hidden behind the natural camouflage of the forest as I neared the small structure. The windows were so dirty I doubted I would be able to see inside. There was a well sitting out back behind the shack. The bucket dangled sideways. On top of the well wall was an old baby doll. Her hair was tangled and full of twigs.

The dress she was wearing looked as though it was once a pretty shade of pink but now faded and dirty. I found myself so intrigued with the place. As I rounded the corner to the front I could see the porch was in really bad shape. Pieces of the wooden floor were missing and there was an old swing hanging that looked as lopsided as the bucket in the well. What once was a yard was now overgrown with wildflowers and other vegetation.

I approached the front door and noticed it wasn't shut all the way. The door knob dangled, matching the rest of the scenery. As I peered through the crack of the door my first view was of a rocking chair. It was facing a fireplace that looked like it hadn't been used in a very long time. There was a window next to the fireplace with no glass. I pushed the door open slowly, presenting more of a view. The wooden floor creaked as I stepped in, the smell was awful and stale. The place seemed to be empty, not that I thought it would be inhabited by anything other than maybe field mice and other varmints. There was what must have been a kitchen area to the right. An old wooden table sat against the exterior wall, there were a few chairs scattered in the general area. Next to the table was a five tier shelf with some dishware and other miscellaneous items. The old wooden stove still had a cast iron tea kettle sitting on it. My eyes fixated on a portrait stuck on the wall of a small child.

It was a little girl who looked to be maybe four or five years old. She was wearing a dress, bonnet and little boots. As I was studying her babyish face, out of the corner of my eye I caught something go by the window next to the fireplace. I stood very still for a moment to look and listen. Nothing.

I walked over to the window to look out but didn't see anything. As I started to turn away something grabbed me by my shoulders and pulled me through the opening! My legs hit the bottom of the sill as I was yanked out. It felt like a small piece of glass stuck in the back of my calf. Whatever had a hold of me was clutching me by the top of my arms so tight I couldn't move and talon like claws were piercing my skin. Meanwhile, my legs continued to dangle under me. I was soaring so fast, getting higher and higher in the sky. I looked to the right and saw a black wing that must have extended eight feet long! I was still screaming. I tried to catch my breath and assess my situation. If this thing dropped me, I would be dead. We were flying over the treetops, going at such a fast pace I could barely turn my head in either direction. My heavy breathing turned into hyperventilating. I soon began feeling light headed and weak. Then…everything went black…

I awoke on the ground, lying face down in the grass. My body feels sore but nothing feels broken. Without raising my head, I turned my eyes upward and saw the most beautiful rainbow in the distance. It extended from one side of a mountain top to the other. The colors were so brilliant... the red, orange, yellow, green, blue, indigo and violet were as vivid as they could be. I looked around and noticed a valley below. My face was burning on one side, it felt like it had scrapes or scratches. Whatever that thing was must have just dropped me here. I turned and looked all around and there was no sign of it anywhere. I got up very slowly and quite awkwardly and took one last look around. Nothing looked familiar so I had no idea which way to go. The shock of everything that had happened was so overwhelming. I felt a numbness, almost as if everything has become too surreal and I couldn't grasp it all. My entire body was shaking but I continued trying to slow my breathing so I would be able to think somewhat clearly. I made the decision to head toward the valley below, my thought was maybe there would be people there. If not, maybe there would at least be water, shelter, trees, some sort of survival elements. My guess was that it would be a lot of walking before reaching the bottom. I had no idea what time it was, but the sun was starting to set so it would be dark soon. I wondered if I should find some sort of cover and just stay put until it was light. After considering my options I decided to put some distance between where I was dumped, even if I hiked down just a mile and found a spot to camp for the night.

The spot I found was alright, with large rocks that I could hide behind, or use to take cover from the wind. I wished I could have continued walking farther that night but I found an area where I could sit with my back against a rock and keep my eyes looking in all three directions. There was not going to be sleep, willingly anyway. I laid down on the cool ground. My eyes continued scanning every area I could see. After only a few minutes I hear what sounded like a man yelling. I realized it WAS someone yelling. Someone was yelling my name and it sounded like my Father. My Father! "Celeste! Celeste!"

"I am here!" I screamed back. The light from the flashlight was getting closer. Thank God. Someone found me! How had they found me in this strange place? The amount of time I had spent at the cabin, wondering and exploring through the woods and had never stumbled across anything like what I saw on this awful visit. My father was running towards me, there were other people with him, including a man in a police uniform, I assumed that is what he was. I could hear him on his radio giving directions, he was telling them that I was behind the cabin. Is he crazy! I must be so far from... then, out of the corner of my eye I saw the cabin! The cabin! How was the cabin there! I was not, and had not been by the cabin for over twenty four hours! There were paramedics running towards me, they started placing gauze on my head.

My head was bleeding. I needed to calm myself, I felt as though I was going to start hyperventilating again. Blood was running down the side of my face. Some of the people were telling me not to close my eyes, to look at them. That's what I was doing, looking all around, wondering how I was back at the cabin, why was I suddenly bleeding so profusely.

I was put onto a stretcher and wheeled quite rapidly toward the front of the cabin. Everyone involved was scurrying about frantically. I felt as though I was floating, every limb was as limber as if they were not even attached. My head was resting on the pillow they had placed down, eyes staring at everything we passed. That's when I noticed my grandfather, lying on the ground, covered in blood. I didn't react. They wheeled me farther down the drive to where the ambulance was parked. I noticed Arnie, lying face down in the path to the barn, not moving. My emotion again, blank, I felt numb. I was put into the back of the ambulance where paramedics began to work on me. I could hear the sirens screaming and feel that we were driving too fast for the poor quality road we were on.

I closed my eyes...

St. Jude Psychiatric Hospital

I awoke to find my hands and feet bound and tied to an old steel framed bed. My five foot six inch frame seemed to be stretched to its limit. I felt very groggy but tried to lift my head to see around the room. There was another steel framed bed against the opposite wall, a dresser in between the two beds and a small door on the wall across from the beds which I assumed was a closet. Other than that the room was empty. The only thing that hung on the wall was a small crucifix above the dresser.

My hair was falling into my mouth and eyes but there was nothing I could do to get it away. Some of my hair was stuck on my forehead, so I assume I had been sweating even though it was rather chilly in the room. I had no blanket. In fact, the only thing I had on was what appeared to be a hospital gown. I laid still and listened for a moment. It was so quiet, I didn't hear a sound, not any voices or noises of any kind.

My eyes began to focus on a spider that was crawling on the ceiling above my head. If it were not for the fact that I was probably heavily drugged, I believe I would have been incredibly anxious about that. Not just because there was a spider directly above my head but also because I had no idea where I was and then there was also the fact that I was bound to a bed! And finally, I can't seem to remember the day before or the day before that. My last memory had been driving to the family cabin. Then, some very mixed up, blurred recollection of events while I was there.

The door to the room going out into a hallway was open. I redirected my eyes and focused on the small section of hallway I could see from where I was. After what seemed like an hour, a lady walked by. I did not yell out to her.

Then about five minutes later she appeared in the doorway. "Well, look who is awake." She said. "My name is Jean. I am a nurse here and I will be helping you during your stay with us."

"I have to use the bathroom." I told her. She looked at me for a few seconds and then started undoing the restraints. Once she had all of them off, she helped me out of the bed. I was very unbalanced and wondered what they had given me. What I thought was a closet was actually a very small bathroom, only a sink and a toilet. A towel hung over the side of the sink and a bar of soap sat by the faucet. When I exited the small bathroom Jean informed me that she was taking me to have breakfast and I needed to follow her. "There you will meet some of the other people that are here."

"Where are my parents? Where am I?" I asked.

"You have just recently been brought to us from a place where you were healing from your injuries. Anyhow, that is not for me to talk to you about, okay, come now. Follow me."

"My injuries?" I inquired.

She stopped walking and looked at me. "Young lady, please. We can talk about all that later. We must get moving."

The room where breakfast was being served was huge. There were a lot of people eating and also some people that were not.

Instead they were either rocking, walking around, sitting on the floor, even rambling things I couldn't understand. One of them rambling was a young man who looked to be my age. He was perched on a window sill staring outside. The noise coming out of his mouth did not form into words, none that I knew anyway. "That's Isaac" Jean said. "He does that often, just to get attention. Usually it is in protest of what we are serving or he is trying to get the other patient's stirred up. Ignore him." She informed me.

Isaac was tall and wiry. He had beautiful thick, brownish hair which was way overdue for a cut. I got caught staring, he turned his head directly at me as if he could sense my eyes on him. His large blue eyes looked friendly, he smiled big and then turned back to looking outside.

Breakfast that morning consisted of waffles, cold scrambled eggs, orange juice, assorted fruit that definitely had come from a can and a vitamin. Nobody talked to me during breakfast. I sat at a table closest to where they were serving up the food. There was a girl sitting at the end of the table when I sat down but she got up and moved right away. Jean came back and sat down across from me at the table when I was almost done eating.

At that point I was beginning to get some wits about me so I asked her again where I was and why. For some reason I wasn't panicked, I'm sure I was still under the influence... of something. She wanted to know what I remembered. I didn't know. I was at the cabin, I recalled swimming and flying, everything was very fuzzy. Jean said the vitamin I took would probably make me tired so we would talk later. She told me I should go back to my room and lie down for a bit. Weird, I thought, I just got up. I was feeling a bit more clear-headed but tired. Off I went to my room as instructed. When I got there I plopped down on the small bed, this time without restraints.

"Hey", a voice came from the hallway. I must have fallen back asleep. I turned my head toward the door and seen that it was the boy from the cafeteria, Isaac.

"Hello", I said.

"Let's go for a walk new girl." Isaac said as he headed over and threw me what looked like a white jogging suit. Same thing he had on. In fact, it looked exactly like what everyone had on. Isaac sat next to me on the bed. "Your day wear new girl. I told the higher ups I would get one to you. You can grab a clean one when needed but try not to make it daily, in the closet at the end of the hallway. Someone has to let you in. Next to the hallway is a shower room, you can only do that with someone supervising.

I would volunteer but they don't let me supervise yet." He smiled big again. "Your nightwear will be placed at the end of your bed and you will get a clean one once a week. Anyway, be very careful not to get either dirty. The workers here do not appreciate dirt. The workers here do not appreciate much of anything."

"Where is here?" I asked.

Isaac smiled again. Then he said, "Welcome to St. Jude Psychiatric Hospital. Where we get treatment for our ailments and also get filled with much useful information. For instance, did you know that twenty-five percent of woman in this country are on medication for mental illness? That is scary! That means seventy-five percent are running around untreated!" Then he laughed at himself like someone else had just told the joke.

"Ha ha, very funny." I said.

Isaac shoved my arm lightly trying to get me to move. I was still trying to take in where I was and why. "A psychiatric hospital?" I questioned.

"Look, I don't know why you are here either. I'll try and get a look at your file sometime, k." Isaac raised his eyebrows at me. I felt like we were late for an appointment.

I jumped up and went into the tiny bathroom with my 'day wear' in hand to get dressed.

The jogging suit was a little on the big size, oh well I thought, better than the hospital gown I had on. When I exited the bathroom Isaac was waiting by the door leading to the hallway waving for me to follow. I walked behind him out into the hallway and down a couple flights of stairs, the whole time making sure we were not spotted by any of the workers. Then, we waited in the stairwell on the bottom floor until the coast was clear, which was swarming with people at the time. All of a sudden, Isaac grabbed my hand, opened the stairwell door, pulled me into the hallway and threw another larger door open, then, we were outside!

The fresh air felt amazing! We began to run through the perfectly manicured lawns, both of us laughing and Isaac was singing some goofy song. I thought we were probably being too loud but I assumed Isaac knew this place better than I did. There was a man trimming a bush by the grand front entrance to the castle like building, he winked at us and smiled as we ran past. I had never seen a building this large in my life! We ran all the way to the back side of the very large structure and it was so beautiful! There were walkways and flowers, bird baths that the birds were landing and flying on and off of. Lots of workers were busily moving about, none seemed to pay any attention to us. I noticed that most had the same white jogging suits as us on, maybe they were patients as well. Isaac slowed his pace and tumbled into the luscious green lawn, I plopped down next to him.

He pulled a handful of candies out of his pocket, we sat, talked and ate candy. Even though I couldn't remember how I ended up in this place I felt like I needed to be here but I wasn't sure why. We must have sat for an hour before Isaac indicated we better get back inside before someone noticed that we were gone.

Entering back through the same door we had snuck out was more terrifying than exiting. We had no idea who was on the other side. Isaac opened the door very slowly, he peered into the small opening to see if it was clear. Both of us were so nervous, I didn't know what would happen if we had gotten caught but I was following Isaac's lead as far as knowing it wouldn't be good. There wasn't any sounds or voices that we could hear coming from the hallway on the other side of the door. Isaac grabbed my hand and we both slid through the door, only opening it far enough for our sideways bodies to get through. Back inside, what a relief!

"We need to get to the dining hall for lunch before they notice us missing." Isaac told me. I nodded my head to let him know I understood and followed him down some hallways until we reached the dining hall. It was pretty full already but there were still people in line to get their food. We snuck into the line quickly, started to talk and act like we had been there the whole time.

There was a nun standing by the wall not too far ahead of where we were. I thought she was giving us a funny look but Isaac assured me that was just how she looked. Lunch on that day consisted of vegetable beef soup, bread, fruit from a can, again, and chocolate pudding.

After lunch everyone was allowed to go to the day room and either play games, put puzzles together, listen to music, or there was a corner that had art supplies; such as pencils, paper, and paint. The art corner was supervised and not everyone could use those items. I tried finding Isaac, we had gotten separated after lunch when one of the workers pulled him aside and did a random search on him. I tried waiting but was yelled at to move on. I could not see him anywhere in the dayroom so I decided to go look for him. I didn't know where his room was or what floor it was on. It seemed like it was all girls down my hall, which was on the second floor so I decided to head up to the third floor. Taking the stairs was a work out but I didn't want anyone to notice that I was running around, I assumed I was supposed to stay in the day room. When I opened the stairwell door I was taken a back with the same nun that I thought was giving Isaac and I funny looks in the dining hall. The nun whipped her head in my direction as soon as she heard the door open. "Well, Well." She said. "If it isn't the other half of the problem I am having today."

She took a couple of steps toward me. "You see, I was told that there were two patients outside earlier today, running amok all around the grounds. I am here to let you know, that kind of behavior is unacceptable!" She took another step and ended up right in front of me, "Not only is it unacceptable but is also punishable by whatever means I deem necessary young lady. Oh and, your friend, Mr. Isaac Dunkin, will be joining you shortly."

Before the last word left her mouth, I was grabbed from behind by two large men, each one grabbed one of my arms and began to lead me down the long hallway. We went up another flight of stairs, down another hallway and finally into a room. The room was large with only a couple of chairs and a steel frame bed, just like the ones we slept on. The men that had a hold of my arms literally picked my feet up off of the floor and threw me on this bed. Then, they grabbed restraints that were hanging down on each side of the steel frame and began to strap me in! These restraints were different than the ones used on me in my room. They went across from one side of the bed to the other, across my head, then my chest, arms, and finally across my legs. I couldn't move at all. One of the men grabbed something off of the cart that sat next to the bed and shoved it in my mouth. It was long and it felt like I was going to choke on it. It tasted like a piece of wood.

I tried to push it out with my tongue but one of the men put his hand on the end of it until I stopped trying. Tears were running down my face, both of the men were ignoring me, instead they were busy messing with some sort of machine that was sitting on the same cart next to the bed that the wooden thing came from. I was trying to figure out what it was or what it was for when I heard Isaac yelling. He was yelling loudly at the scary looking nun that had entered with him. Isaac was in some sort of straight jacket that had his arms strapped in tight. He was telling the nun not to hurt me, that it wasn't my fault, to punish him and not me. Then, those men were putting electrode looking things on my head. The whole thing was terrifying. Isaac was making it worse by all of his screaming, it was making me that much more nervous about what was about to happen. The nun appeared on the side of the bed and was staring down at me with a look of disgust on her face. She lifted her head and moved her eyes across the top of me to one of the large men standing on the other side of the bed and nodded. Without warning, a shock went through me. My body began convulsing, then stop, then start up again. This continued until I must have passed out. I don't know how long it went on for after that.

I awoke back in my bed and felt quite sick and nauseated so I laid still for a while. The last thing I remembered was lying on a bed in a large room in restraints and Isaac yelling. I remembered the scary nun looking down at me.

My thoughts were swimming when I heard a noise coming from the other side of the room. It sounded like someone crying very softly. I rolled over and saw a girl, she looked to be about my age, sitting on the bed across from mine. She was facing my way but had her head looking down toward the floor. "Hey," I said softly. She didn't respond so I said it once more.

She raised her head and looked up at me. "Hey," she said back.

"What's your name?" I asked.

"Kora," She replied.

"I'm Celeste. Did you just get here?"

"I think so," she said. "I can't seem to remember much of anything though." I felt exactly the same. My mind was foggy. I was having memories that weren't complete and I wasn't sure when they were from or if they were even real.

"It is time for dinner." A very firm voice said from the doorway. Kora looked at whoever was standing there but I just stayed the way I was and didn't move at all. I was looking at Kora. I noticed her eyes getting bigger and then suddenly my head was jerked back with great force. I recognized the voice to be the nun who had taken me and Isaac to the large room. She had a hold of my hair and was pulling it so hard that my face was looking up at the ceiling. "You will look at me when I am addressing you young lady." I tried to nod to let her know I understood but she was holding on so tightly I couldn't move my head at all.

With that, she let go and left the room. Kora ran over to me to see if I was alright.

"We better get to the dining hall," I said.

I hadn't seen Isaac since we were in that awful room together. I wanted to know if he was alright. After scanning the dining hall for a moment I noticed him sitting at a table by himself over by one of the large windows. Oh thank God, I thought. He looked my way and I gave a slight wave to let him know that I saw him. I told Kora about Isaac, whom I just met, and the fun we had that afternoon running around all over the grounds. I also told her that we were punished for doing that. We were speaking softly as to not bring any un-wanted attention to ourselves. Unwritten rules seemed to float in the air at this place, one was supposed to know them as well as the written ones, and to also understand that the rules could be changed at any time. There were nuns everywhere and they all wore the same hateful look on their faces. We got our portion of meat covered in a soupy gravy with mashed potatoes, green beans, fruit cocktail, and what I'm assuming was pineapple upside down cake.

Kora and I were making our way over to where Isaac was sitting when one of the patients got up from his table and jumped right in front of us. He started screaming so loud it startled us both.

He took a step toward us and as Kora stepped back she lost control of her tray and dropped it to the floor. Food went flying everywhere. Two of the men workers were making their way toward us, when they reached us they grabbed the man and started dragging him kicking and yelling out of the dining hall. One of the nuns was also making her way toward us. She raised her hand and slapped Kora across the face with such force it knocked her glasses to the ground. "Stupid girl!" She yelled. "You will clean every last bit of this up! Then you can sit and watch everyone else eat. You will go to bed hungry and the next time you are walking with a tray of food you might be more careful." I felt like screaming at this nun and telling her it wasn't Kora's fault but I knew it wouldn't matter. That would have just led to more punishment for us. I am learning quickly how things are going to be here.

Once Kora was done cleaning the mess up, she came and joined Isaac and I at the table. I was eating slowly so that I could save some food to sneak to her. We were very careful not to get caught giving her small bites of food. I can't imagine what the punishment would have been for that. The three of us spent the rest of the time talking and trying to understand how we all ended up in this place. Our memories were all messed up, missing pieces or totally not there at all. Isaac remembered the most but he had been here the longest.

He said things were starting to come back to him, things he wasn't ready to share just yet. He told us that his counselor here would make him talk about it. The more he talked the more memories would come flooding in. I wondered if that would happen with me. Then the already familiar sound of the bells started to ring indicating it was time to leave the dining hall. There were nuns and staff standing by all of the trash cans and tables that you were to set your tray on to make sure you had ate everything.

Minutes turned into hours and hours turned into days, days turned into weeks. Before I realized it I had been at this strange place for a month. Some of our memories were very clear and yet others still so disheveled. In that month, Kora, Isaac and I had gotten to know and trust each other very well. I have learned that Kora was from Salem, Massachusetts. Isaac was born in Detroit Michigan but has lived in many places, his family moved around a lot. Isaac said his father was very anti-government and at times they had even lived in communal type places. Kora said that she didn't know her father but did know he was of African American descent since her mother was as white as snow and she is dark skinned, has big beautiful brown eyes and curly black hair. From what I could remember, my upbringing seemed pretty normal compared to theirs, that was, until right before I got here.

I was starting to remember some and also had a strong feeling that something really bad had happened to me. One of the questions that mostly Isaac and I had and spoke of is why our families never came to see us. One would think that if they were aware of our predicament that they would surely come and take us out of this awful place. We had asked that question many times and were never given a direct answer. We were told that our families have chosen to try and forget the horrible events we put them through, seeing us would not allow them to forget.

Kora and I shared a room. Isaac was on the third floor but we were together as much as possible. The three of us ate our meals together and spent the rest of the hours of the days in sync. We had laughs watching the outdated movies the staff would allow us to view once a week for a treat and we had become each other's family in our new dysfunctional home.

The place we called home was four stories high but also had a basement. The basement was always off limits and always guarded. It had long hallways on the second, third and fourth floor that harbored lots of patients. Each one dealing with their own personal demons and sicknesses. The main level contained many offices, the huge dining hall and the day room, which was also huge.

There were some buildings on the property that were disconnected from where we lived and I assumed they were used for many things. Maybe one was where the nuns gathered to summon the demons that possessed them. Maybe another was where they hid the slaves that kept this place looking so inviting to the uninformed outside world. Actually, many of the patients were allowed to 'work'. Those who remained in a trance like state and didn't give the nuns reason to 'punish' them. Some were even allowed outside. Isaac would joke that they kept offering him a job but the pay sucked so he had to continually turn them down. I'm not sure how Isaac kept his sense of humor but I am so thankful he did. Kora could be defiant and that worried me. She would behave as though she had forgotten where we were. I would remind her often. I felt like I was pretty level headed but then there were days I felt I just didn't have the energy to be.

There had been punishments for all three of us during the last month, I think the workers and nuns were the crazy ones. At times we willfully decided an hour of fresh air with the smells that came from being outside was worth the hours of torture we would undoubtedly endure. The worst infliction I have had so far has to have been the bath. I was caught trying to sneak a piece of bread out of the dining hall.

My intentions were to give it to Isaac who had all meals of that day taken away. I can't even recall why Isaac was being punished but my punishment for trying to feed a hungry friend was to get into a cold bath, where I stayed for two days straight, sitting in cold water the entire time. My body would start to shake so badly the cover that had been put over the top of the tub with just my head sticking out of a hole would vibrate intensely. Another one of their methods of abuse was being wrapped tightly with cold towels. Kora had been wrapped on more than one occasion for eight hours each time. According to some of the other residents, that was not that bad, they told us it could have been much longer. I don't think the people here who are suffering from some sort of mental illness understood what was going on, they had no idea why they were being punished.

We are also all going to therapy sessions, group and individual. During these sessions all three of us seemed to be recovering some of our memories. I can recall the screams coming from the couch that the patient would sit on in the individual therapy room, and the realization that the screams where coming from me.

It was nearing the end of yet another month. Kora had been in individual therapy all one morning.

When Isaac and I first seen her she was running past the day room doorway. We looked at each other and at the same time stood up from where we were sitting to go after her. Kora bolted right out the front door of St. Jude. Without hesitation, Isaac and I followed. We found her sitting on the steps of the massive front porch rocking violently back and forth. She turned in our direction. "I remember! I remember everything!" She screamed.

Witch

Kora began telling us her story.

Growing up in Salem, Massachusetts was great. I was very interested in the history of the town I was born into. I was raised by my mother, never knew my father.

We lived in a small house in a quiet neighborhood, the houses were few and far between. My mother was a guide, a guide for people who wanted to know what happened so many years ago in our town. Some of the locals referred to mother as a witch, she referred to herself as clairvoyant. Mother had many clients that were local but the majority were tourists. They would come from far away to see her, so excited to see this visionary woman go into a trance like state and be possessed by a soul from long ago. For them it was like a visit from the past. A peek into the thoughts and feelings of a person who had lived long ago or even not so long ago. My mother had been doing that for people, for as long as I could remember. My growing up years were pretty normal, I thought anyway. I always worked as much as I could to help out with my own expenses so I wouldn't be too much of a burden, not that I ever got the impression that I was. But, my mother was the only person in our home with an income. I started to work when I was quite young with babysitting jobs and then moved into waitressing once I was in high school.

It was my senior year of high school. I was looking into what colleges to apply to along with the rest of my classmates. At the time that the most horrible thing of my life was about to happen, I was looking forward to our school's annual Harvest Dance. My girlfriends and I had planned a shopping trip to Marblehead.

A town only about fifteen minutes from Salem known to have the best boutique for the kind of dresses we wanted for the dance. It was a formal event and we fully intended on treating it that way.

The day started early. Elizabeth picked me up at eight that morning. Nancy was already with her so we headed out, stopping first at the local 'Waffle House' restaurant for breakfast before leaving town. Besides, the Boutique didn't open until nine, so we had time to spare.

Entering the Boutique was incredible. The most beautiful dresses were hanging in rows. Some were long and flowing, and others short. There were dresses that shimmered and there were some that stood alone in their own elegance. We spent hours in the store trying on a countless number of dresses. I finally decided I had found the absolute perfect one. It was tangerine in color and it came all the way to the floor. The top part of the dress was fitted and sparkled in the light with every move I made. I remember it perfectly. I felt like a princess. The price tag was a bit startling but I had been saving for this shopping trip for a while. I was putting half of the tips I was making from the diner away knowing I was going to buy the perfect dress for this dance. After all, it was my senior year. Never again would I be doing some of these things. "You look so beautiful Kora." Nancy said.

"I love it." I responded excitedly. We paid for our dresses and left to go have lunch.

After lunch, we made a few more stops before heading home. It had been a very successful day. All of us found our perfect dress and had lots of fun doing it. And the day wasn't over, we still had plans to go to the movies but first needed to stop at my house to put our dresses in my room so they weren't sitting in the car. I warned Elizabeth and Nancy to be quiet going in because there was a strange car in the drive which meant mother had a client. We crept through the house up to my room being as quiet as we could. Then I left a note on the refrigerator which was mother's rule that said, MOVIES.

We chose to go to a scary one, our favorite genre. I remember it being pretty bad. A vampire thriller with bad acting and an obvious story line.

Elizabeth dropped me at the end of my drive after the movies. The air was cool that night. The walk to our small house wasn't too long but you couldn't see the house until rounding a corner in the driveway. I was walking at a pretty fast pace, I had only put a light cardigan on and I was cold. When the house came into view the car that was there when we dropped the dresses off was still there. I thought that was strange. Mother's appointments never lasted that long. She said it took too much out of her.

As I approached the front door I could hear voices. One of them was my mother's, the other was male. They weren't quite yelling but were certainly raised. I decided to go around to the back of the house and enter into the kitchen so I didn't disturb them in case this was about the message the client had received. Some of the people that came to see mother were descendants of the witches that were hung during the trials and could get upset and shook up about what they found out. I opened the door slowly to minimize the creaking sound it made when you opened it and tiptoed through the kitchen to get a view of who was in the other room. There was a large black male sitting on one of the chairs with his hands on his head. He looked to be around my mother's age. My mother was pacing back and forth. I tried to stay out of sight so I could continue to listen to the conversation. "I just want to be able to see her." The stranger said. My mother turned and walked back his way ending up right in front of him.

She bent down a bit and said in a low voice, "You knew damn well the choice you made seventeen years ago. I told you what your options were. The fact that I have continued this charade with you for all these years is bad enough." The man looked up at my mother, he looked as though he was getting angry.

He spoke loudly, "I am a married man Jan. You knew that and have known that for the last seventeen years! You knew the deal as well. I never once told you I had any intention of leaving my wife.

But the fact remains, we had a daughter together. A daughter I have only seen from a distance."

What was this man talking about? I was trying to understand what was being said. He said a daughter, but I'm an only child. This is craziness I thought. Was this my father!

My mother's voice interrupted my thoughts. "I knew alright. I knew you were never going to be a father to your daughter. How could you be? So what would have been the point of ever knowing anything about her? I recall you and I having many meetings in these last seventeen years and you weren't concerned with asking about our daughter at those." With that, the man stood and got in my mother's face. I was shocked and nervous, I didn't know what to do. I tried so hard to not start crying but was unsuccessful. Once I started I could feel myself began to shake. I quickly put my hands up to my mouth to prevent noise from escaping. This failed because all of a sudden a small whimper came out and instantly my mother and the man turned in my direction.

The man was moving toward the kitchen so fast I didn't have time to react. My mother was right behind him. "You stay away from her!" She screamed. The man reached into the back of his pants and pulled out a gun and pointed it at my mother. I began screaming at the top of my lungs, he turned and grabbed my arm. I remember him squeezing my arm so hard, at the same time yelling at me to shut up.

"I'm not going to hurt you girl!" He said. My mother was punching the man in the head and anywhere else she could land one until he got a hold of her and literally threw her across the room. I jerked my arm free and ran to her side. The man's breathing was quick and forceful. He had the gun pointed in our direction. He spoke softly, "Enough of this. Both of you get up and go into the garage." I was sobbing, I didn't know what he was going to do next. Once in the garage he kept the gun pointed in our direction and instructed me to open the trunk. My mother was pleading with him not to do whatever it was he was thinking. Her plea's fell on deaf ears, he continued with his demands until both my mother and I were in the trunk of her car. The trunk slammed down with a thunderous sound.

I could feel the car when it began to move. The trunk was so dark. I could sense that we were moving through the neighborhoods going around corners and then speeding up as we went onto the Interstate. It felt as though we were moving fast and the motion of the car behaved like we were moving in and out of traffic. I began to kick, trying to knock anything out to create a hole. Kicking at the brake lights and the top of the trunk itself just thinking maybe it would pop open. My mother was trying to talk to me but I wouldn't calm down. Finally, she grabbed my arm and asked that I please listen. "When we get to where we are going," she said, I am going to distract him and I want you to run. You run as fast and as far as you can Kora. You run for your life!"

"I'm not leaving you." I told her. Then, the car made a violent turn. It was so sharp I ended up rolling on top of my mother, we struggled to get back into a position so that we would at least not be on top of each other. We could tell that we were now on some kind of back country, unpaved roadway. It had gotten very bumpy and we were flopping all around. We stayed on this uneven road for quite a long time until finally the car took another swift turn and then came to an abrupt stop.

Suddenly, the trunk flung open. It was very dark out. The man ordered us out of the trunk and into an old hunting blind he had parked next to. There was no time for distractions or running, everything had happened so fast from the trunk opening and us being shoved into the blind. There were two chairs inside and a kerosene lamp that was tipped over on the ground, along with a dirty flannel shirt. The man shoved my mother onto one of the chairs and pushed me by my shoulders to the ground to sit. He picked the other chair up, spun it around, and sat on it backwards. "Let's get started." He said. "This has been a long time coming. Kora, I am sure you have figured out by now that I am your father, and this is truth. I wish things could have been different all these years and I would have been able to be a father to you but that was not possible.

I have thought about you all these years though and I have wanted to at least give you one thing, an important thing, knowledge. What I would like to do is start with your mother sharing some things with you about her past. I know you have thought poorly of me all you're growing up years, thinking of me as a deadbeat dad I am sure, which was not entirely true. And now, I would like your mother to share with you why I am concerned about you. I have watched you at times from a distance. I saw what you did one day, you have powers Kora. I saw what you did. I am a God fearing man and I don't want any kin of mine to practice this hocus pocus. It has bothered me for a long time the way you are being brought up, outside of the church. Being taught evil. Your mother has a rather powerful gift and she used this gift to seduce me She wanted a child, I gave her a child. There are things she has never shared with you, she is going to share those things with you now Kora, yes indeed. Because these sort of things get passed down, so if this power has been passed onto you, you have the right to know. Maybe spend time trying to figure it out so you will use it for good and not evil." He turned and looked at my mother. "I didn't plan on doing this today, but it is happening, so, start from the beginning Jan. And don't leave anything out."

If my mother's eyes could have burned a hole in the man's heart, he certainly would have been dead.

She shifted her focus to me and after a few moments of silence she began to speak softly.

"Our family has lived in Salem for centuries as you know. We too have ancestors that were here during the trials. On my mother's side, a woman named Delilah, it would be many great grandmothers to you, lived here in Salem and there had been an accusation made of witchery toward her. As there were against so many others at that time. Delilah was probably twenty six years old at this time, and the mother of two children. Her husband had been killed a year earlier in a hunting accident. She was raising her children on her own just outside of town working as a midwife to support her family.

On a dark, rainy evening in the middle of summer a young man came to her home asking for help. He was frantic and insisted that Delilah come with him to help his wife. He told Delilah that he moved his wife into a cabin in the woods outside of town hoping to escape the mayhem going on with all of the accusations of witchcraft, mostly happening right in the village. Delilah grabbed her small bag and ran out the front door with the stranger, instructing her children to stay at home and she would return soon. Once arriving at the small cabin the man had set up as their homestead, Delilah could hear a woman's screams coming from inside. The man was running ahead now instructing for Delilah to hurry. When they got inside, Delilah could see the woman was clearly in labor. She went into action, instructing the husband to boil some water, bring fresh towels and then to go outside and wait.

Delilah could barely get the poor girl to focus. She continued screaming and crying for the next hour until finally it became time to deliver the baby. Delilah was giving instruction for the girl to start pushing. The experienced midwife could tell right away that the baby was breech. Things became frantic in the small cabin with both woman wanting this baby out quickly. The young girl was doing all she could to push the baby out, using every last ounce of energy she had left in her. Finally, the baby was out far enough that Delilah could grab hold and help by pulling gently. Not long after that, the newborn was in Delilah's arms and she quickly wrapped the towel around the small baby girl. Delilah noticed something was wrong immediately, the newborn was not taking breath. Delilah stuck her finger in the baby's mouth and did a sweep to try and clear anything that may be disrupting her airway, nothing happened. She then gave the baby a pinch to see if that would cause any reaction, nothing happened. Delilah tried to give the baby breath by breathing into her mouth and continued this for some time. The baby lay limp in her arms. She looked up at the young girl who couldn't have been more than fifteen years of age.

The young girl was still trying to catch her breath and compose herself. Delilah handed her the newborn baby girl. The young mother stared down at her daughter for a few moments not moving her eyes from her babies tiny, still body. Her breathing became heavy and she had began to cry. "Why does she not move or make sound?" She asked. Delilah explained that her baby was born with no life in her, told the young mother how sorry she was. The young girl became hysterical. Delilah left the room to go and deliver the sad news to the young man who had been waiting outside. Before Delilah could finish her last statement the young man brushed past her and ran into the cabin. Delilah sat down on an old chair sitting by the front door, she was exhausted from the whole ordeal but wanted to wait and see if the young couple needed any more assistance before leaving. After a time when no one came out she decided to head home.

Once home, she checked on her children who were soundly sleeping, thanked God for them and went to lay down to try and get some rest.

Morning came quickly. Delilah was up preparing breakfast when she heard voices outside somewhere in the distance. She went to the small window by her front door and saw a large group of people from the village heading toward her house.

She quietly opened the front door and stepped out to await them and see what was going on. When the group got near she could see that the older man in the front was John Gidon, the minister from the church Delilah and her children attended every Sunday. Walking right beside him was the young couple from that very night before, the ones who had just lost their baby girl. The group reached the front of Delilah's home and stopped.

John spoke first, "Delilah Elizabeth Foster?" He spoke as if this was a question.

"Yes. You know who I am John."

John took a step forward and cleared his throat. "You are here by being charged with the crime of stealing the breath from new life, witnessed by the child's own mother. One can assume the only way for you to have the power to do such a thing is none other than the fact that you have been practicing in dark magic, making deals with the devil himself. Witchcraft!"

Delilah who was standing frozen in the same spot since the group arrived couldn't believe her ears. She looked the group over and was befuddled at who had come to accuse her of such things. They were all town's people she had considered friends, people she had helped whenever they needed her services.

"Do you deny this?" John yelled.

Delilah stood tall and spoke, "I deny these allegations wholeheartedly, I have never nor would ever do the things that you say I have.

I am your neighbor, I would not harm an innocent or anyone for that matter. You people know that of me. I tried everything I could to help your granddaughter's baby John."

John took another step forward and looked Delilah right in the eyes and said to her, "It is such a strange time we are living in right now. Good folk that are now doing things they never thought possible, but the devil has come to Salem and he is feasting on the weak. We need to be strong and uncompromising in our values and beliefs so not to be entranced by the demons that have invaded our village. You yourself just witnessed another one of our neighbors who had been provoked and tempted by one of these demons. Can you deny that the woman you knew as a good wife and mother was no longer behaving as such? These demons will lie to us and try and make us believe that nothing is different, when we know and realize it is. The crime you have committed deserves no trial, for to deny a newborn their first breath in this world is the worst kind of evil. For these reasons Delilah I am not only charging but convicting you with the crime of witchcraft, punishable by death!" Two of the men walked quickly to grab hold of Delilah, one on each arm and proceeded to lead her by force back toward the village. Before her home was completely out of sight Delilah heard the cries of her children.

"Mother!" They were yelling. She turned to look at them but the gentleman on her right grabbed her under her chin and jerked her face back forward.

The walk ended on the edge of town where she was forced into a makeshift holding place. It was a man-made hole in the earth. The two men threw her in and then placed a heavy piece of wood on top that had holes cut into it. Delilah collapsed to the dirt ground and began to pray. She had her eyes closed and continued praying until she heard a voice "Our God is stronger than the demon you pray to you know." Delilah looked up and saw the young girl who delivered a dead baby the night before staring down at her. She must have been the one that told these lies to the townspeople. The young girl was glaring with such a look of hatred and said "You are going to die just like my baby died when you took her breath from her. I am going to watch as we take your breath from you." Then her young husband appeared next to her. He looked so distraught. He seemed to look at Delilah with a look of sorrow, and then, took his wife by the hand and led her away. The dirt in the hole Delilah settled in was cold. Every once in a while someone would come by to condemn or spit into the hole saying awful things as they did so.

By morning, Delilah had pretty much accepted her fate, so now she prayed for her children, that they be spared in all of this and that a good family would take them in and provide for their needs.

In the early morning hours a small group of people came to take Delilah out of the hole. Because she had already been found guilty without a trial, her death would happen right away. Town folk were looking for immediate retribution being that it was a brand new life that had been taken. They led her up a hill near the center of town to a large tree that was standing all alone. Most of the townspeople were there, gathered around as if they were waiting for Sunday service. Delilah could see the rope that was hanging from one of the large branches swaying in the wind. Moments later, after some words from a few people, including John who had the final words of damnation, the noose was placed on Delilah's neck, she took one last look at everything around her and had time for one last thought of her children. She felt complete sadness and helplessness. Two men, whom she had known her entire life, raised her up about ten feet off the ground. Her petite body struggled for a short time and then went limp until there was no life left in her."

When my mother was telling the story she wasn't really looking at me, it was as if she was seeing it, reliving it as she spoke. I was sobbing when she got done.

Then the man who had us held captive stood up. "Very good Jan. The rest of the story goes something like this. You see, ever since that day in Salem, Delilah's children and their children and so on were determined to get their revenge on the puritans of that time. If not them directly, then their descendants. Your mother is a descendant of dear Delilah, and so are you Kora. I have been doing a lot of thinking and soul searching recently. I think because you will both spend your life time focused on revenge and bringing misery to others, and I am aware of this, then it is my obligation to spare anyone else that may be affected by the evil that runs through your blood line." My mother had a look of complete fear on her face. She started to plea with this man, my father, as weird as that sounded. I was in complete shock, it felt as though I was having an out of body experience, like I was witnessing all of this happening, things were spiraling out of control and I couldn't do anything to stop it.

My mother was talking, "Please Cecil, you said you were concerned for Kora, you said you weren't going to hurt her, what are you doing? You have stopped taking your medication again, you aren't thinking clearly. My daughter didn't even know her ancestry. I am not interested in getting revenge against anyone."

"Our daughter Jan! Our daughter!" He screamed. My mother tried to speak again but he shouted over her. "I am not going to listen to anything else you have to say! You have tried to hurt me and now I realize so will she, just give it time! My thoughts have never been clearer. This is going to end and it is going to end today, it is going to end right now." My heart was in my throat as he grabbed my mother around her neck. She struggled to get free and they ended up on the ground of the blind we were in. The man grabbed a knife from his front pocket and began to jab it into my mother over and over again. I sprung up and jumped on this man's back, punching and screaming. He threw me off but I got back up, desperately trying to get his hand and stop the attack. I was able to get to the side of the man's head and bit down on his ear as hard as I could, which made him drop the knife. I reached and grabbed it before he even realized where it had landed. I began to stab the man repeatedly, anywhere and everywhere, wildly jabbing the knife into him until he fell to his side. I put the knife in him several more times as he lay there not moving. Then, I sat on my knees with my chest rising and falling heavily as I tried to catch my breath. I kept my eyes on this man for at least a couple of minutes to make sure he wasn't going to move. I looked at my mother and could tell that she was dead. I felt really light headed, my entire body went tingly and numb. I must have passed out.

When I came to I was outside of the blind. I looked around and had no idea where I was. I didn't want to leave my mother lying dead in the same place with the monster who killed her but I was panicked and in a state of shock I imagine. I wanted to run, I wanted to get far away from that place. I got into my mother's car that was parked right next to the blind, started it and put the gas pedal to the floor. I noticed my arms were covered in blood, then looked down and noticed my entire body was drenched in it. I didn't know if any of it was mine, I didn't know the road I was on or where it led to. I didn't know if I was going in the same direction we came in on so I could get back out. I know I did not let up on the gas. The last thing I remember is coming up to a sharp curve in the road.

Memories and Time

Isaac and I were sitting in disbelief from what Kora had just told us. "The next thing I knew", she said, "I was waking up here at this place." She looked at me and Isaac and then turned her attention toward the large lawn in front of us. My first thoughts were sadness and fear thinking about someone, especially someone I knew and cared about, going through that. But then a strange feeling came over me, the fact that Kora had been through something so terrifying helped me in a way, it made me feel like I wasn't alone.

With my memories of the cabin and the shack becoming quite clear, I knew I had been through something horrific as well. We sat for a while longer on the giant front steps and Isaac and I both tried to comfort and help with our words. Then decided we had better get back in before someone noticed our absence if they haven't already. If they had, we had grown so accustomed to the punishments it was almost an expected weekly activity anyway.

We had managed to creep back into the building unscathed for the moment. Later that evening we would not be so lucky. Kora and I had snuck into

Isaac's room after quiet time. Quiet time was just that, in your room, preferably in bed by nine P.M. And you certainly were not allowed to leave the room. Kora and I were going back and forth sharing our memories, almost like we were now kindred spirits that finally had come together to share and talk and try to make sense of the things that had happened to us and maybe, just maybe, some sort of healing might take place." So was it Arnie who shot you or your grandpa?" Isaac asked me again.

"It was Arnie." I said. "The memory I have of being shot is still not real clear, it hasn't come back like the rest of the memories from that day. I don't think Arnie wanted to take the chance of leaving me alive after I knew what was going on with him and grandpa. I guess grandpa must have caught up with Arnie just in time or stumbled upon us in time, I can't really recall that part yet.

What I do know is that both Arnie and grandpa are dead. The police said they thought what happened was Arnie shot me, then at the same time, Arnie and grandpa shot each other." We were talking about our personal nightmares as if we were telling a story about something we seen on the news. I think the medications, otherwise known as vitamins, we were fed daily helped keep us "calm" as Isaac would say.

Without warning, the door to Isaac's room flung open, it startled all three of us. It was one of the very unhappy, wretched, bad-tempered nuns. You could never guess what the punishment was going to be for breaking a rule, they liked to keep the form of abuse unpredictable, they were full of new and impressive ways to make one suffer.

I could hear Kora's screams as I lay on a flat table wrapped in freezing cold towels. Every so often, one of the nuns would walk through, grab a large cup full of freezing cold water and pour it onto the towel from my neck to my toes. My entire body would react with a form of shock from the cold. I hated them, the nuns, they were supposed to be committed to helping others, what a lie they live, at least the ones here! My body couldn't control the shivering, I felt like I was freezing. Kora's screams subsided after a time and I became numb to the cold.

I didn't know if my body was still shivering, I didn't know how long I had been wrapped and strapped to the uncomfortable table. Sometimes, you would lose track of time during these cruel mistreatments.

The next morning Isaac, Kora and I started to talk about and plan our escape. We were all going to be eighteen years old soon. We should be able to find work and a place to rent and leave this dreadful place behind us forever. The plan... was the one thing we enjoyed talking about most. Every day we talked about escaping. Just the thought alone that it may happen was so exciting. It was winter and the grounds were covered in a blanket of snow. We all agreed it would not be a good time to escape. The air was cold day and night and we knew that it could take some time before finding a place to live, which meant possibly sleeping outside for some time. Whatever we had to do would be better than things were for us here in this hell on earth.

There was another possibility that was discussed. I had a cousin who was only a couple years older than me. Maybe we could stay with her for a while. Her name is Sophie, I had started to write her but never heard anything back and my guess was that the letters never got sent. None of us ever had visits from family, old friends, no one. It had gotten to the point that we really didn't want to face our family at all.

Seeing family at this point seems like it would dredge up emotions that had already been worked through or had been buried very deep. None of us could figure out the reason that we had been forgotten but had adopted an attitude of it was us against the world. Besides, how could our families have allowed us to stay in such an awful place? They must have agreed, signed us in, we were all minors. I didn't know if Sophie had a place of her own or really anything about what was going on with her at this point. It might be worth looking her up when the time came though.

Another month went by and it had been two weeks since we had seen Isaac. He was drug out of the day room one afternoon because he had been singing and running through the hallways, he really enjoyed doing that. Sister Ann Marie caught up with him in the day room where she proceeded to grab his ear lobe, squeeze as hard as she could and direct him out. We have all been MIA at times for days but never this long. Kora and I were getting worried. Wondering what kind of torture he must have been going through was awful for us, and no doubt worse for him. The next day late in the afternoon Kora and I were sitting in the sunroom, the one that the residents were allowed in, when a young man walked in. His face was badly swollen, he had bruises down both arms and there was still some dried up blood on his hands and splotches on other parts of his body and clothing.

It took Kora and I both a couple of minutes before realizing it was Isaac who we were looking at.

"We are leaving right now!" Kora said. She got up from the chair she was sitting on and grabbed Isaac and I by our arms and continued walking out of the room. She drug us behind her for a bit down the hallway, then dropped our arms. Kora whipped around, her eyes had a wide and determined look. "Say good-bye to this house of horrors my friends. Forever! I have a plan, well kind of, a spontaneous one anyway. We need to get into the kitchen area." Isaac and I exchanged looks because that was not going to be an easy task. The kitchen area was filled with workers, nuns, therapists, teachers, just about anyone who had any business at St. Jude's could be in the kitchen at any time.

"Kora I don't know if that is a good idea. Remember the time we snuck in to steal brownies? I felt that punishment for a week." I reminded her.

"We won't get caught this time." Isaac said and then continued. "We are on a mission this time, it is do or die time ladies. I say we do before the latter happens."

"Hey guys?" I said. "Why are we going to the kitchen?"

Kora had already started walking, she turned my way and quietly said, "There is money in the kitchen."

The three of us continued the walk toward the kitchen. It was in between meal times so hopefully that would help, maybe some workers would be on break.

As we approached the staff door we could look through the glass window. Isaac put his face right up to the window and looked as far as he could in each direction. He turned and looked at Kora and me and whispered "I can see one lady washing dishes off to the right. I can't see that well through the small window. We are going to have to go in." My heart began to pound so loudly I could hear it beating in my ears. Isaac slowly opened the door, just a small crack at first then a few more inches and stopped to listen, then a little more until we could fit through. The lady washing dishes was being loud enough that our footsteps wouldn't be noticed. We didn't seem to have any kind of plan, other than getting into the kitchen without being seen. We needed a distraction so that we could make it to the back door. I noticed a large shelving unit straight ahead that had a number of pots and pans sitting on it. I tapped Isaac on the shoulder to get his attention. I pointed out the shelving unit to Isaac and Kora. They both nodded, I assumed they understood what I was thinking. We looked over where the lady was washing dishes and she was still washing away. There was music playing farther down in the large kitchen area. The door to the huge walk in freezer, at the far end of the kitchen area, opened and another worker came out with two big boxes of some sort of frozen entrees in his hand. Thank goodness these boxes came up to his eyes so he couldn't really focus on anything in the room but where he was planning on setting the boxes down.

Kora pointed to the left, we could see there were employee jackets and purses hanging on hooks on the wall in a small area that led to an outside entrance for the kitchen workers. It would have been locked from the outside requiring workers to have keys to get in, but it wouldn't be locked from the inside... I hoped. I gestured toward the shelving unit and with my hands tried to let Isaac and Kora know we needed to act now, before it was too late and we found ourselves caught. They both nodded. I took the lead. I was so nervous it felt like my heart was in my throat making it hard to swallow. We reached the tall shelving unit quick, noticed it wasn't hooked to the wall or anything. Perfect I thought. I was standing right next to the shelves and I kind of froze, just standing there looking around. I noticed Isaac reach up as far as he could reach, he grabbed a pole on the unit and pulled as hard as he could, the whole thing came forward, pots and pans started falling and crashing to the floor. It took just a few steps to get where the coats and purses hung, all three of us were in that back area by the exit before anyone so much as turned around.

We could hear someone yell, "What the hell!"

Each of us had our hands in purses and coat pockets taking any cash we found, keeping our ears open for anyone noticing us. We moved quickly, listening to the few workers scrambling to pick up pans, blaming each other for running into the unit. We need to be out of the building by the time they figured out that it was not each other.

Then, we heard the voice we all probably feared the most, Sister Mary Margaret. She had single handedly been responsible for the majority of our pain and suffering. Kora grabbed at us and waved toward the door. Isaac got to the door first, turned the knob slowly, began to push, and it started to open. It wasn't locked! It made a creaking noise that sounded like a semi-truck running into the building to us. Once all three of us were outside, standing on the steps, was the first time I felt like I could take a breath since we entered the kitchen.

"Let's hug the building and head as far away from the front entrance as we can. Then sprint through the yard to the woods out back." Isaac said. We agreed and started to move.

"Wait." Kora exclaimed. She headed back up the steps and with a look of pain on her face, closed the door we had just exited.

"Let's go." I said with a very shaky voice. Moments later we were running across the grounds, which still had small amounts of snow in some areas, heading toward the woods at the edge of the property. We were constantly looking behind us fully expecting a group of people to be chasing us, possibly with weapons in hand ready to beat the devil out of us one last time. Nobody was. When we reached the edge of the property where the lawn and trees formed a perfect line we all turned back almost at the same time and took one last look at St. Jude.

We all paused, it was a melancholy moment. "I hope to never see you again." I said

"Come on, let's keep moving." Isaac said.

We didn't stop walking for hours, heading deeper and deeper into the woods. We had come across a small creek where we stopped to rest and drink some of the clean, cold water. It was cool out, probably only in the fifty degree range and none of us had a coat or any extra clothing. This was not the way our escape plan we talked of so often went. But, it ended up being such a spontaneous thing that we were just happy we got out. We also took this opportunity to empty our pockets and see what kind of cash we ended up with. Between the three of us we managed to get a total of just under two hundred dollars. I didn't think that was going to last very long and it brought about a feeling of panic. I took some long deep breaths to try and calm myself down, it was working. We will figure something out, we had to.

The conversation between us turned into trying to figure out where we were. We were pretty sure we knew that we were in Lower Michigan somewhere. That realization was made because of several things we had noticed. One being that almost all of the license plates we had seen were Michigan. The other was one of the nurses who worked at St. Jude's had told us that is where we were, and finally we had seen the address on a piece of mail that was sitting on a desk in Sister Mary Margaret's office. The only part showing on the letter in the address section was Michigan and a zip code, there was another piece of mail covering the rest. But even with all of that we still did not know what city we were in. What we did know was that we wanted to get to the Upper Peninsula. Different people at St. Jude's had talked of the Upper Peninsula, had told us about its beauty and referred to it as 'God's Country'. The most important part of us wanting to go there was the fact that we were told you could get lost forever up there, it was like its own little universe, disconnected in a way from the rest of the world. That is exactly where we needed to be!

I was sure that the staff at St. Jude had noticed that we were missing by now. I wasn't sure how they would have handled the situation and don't recall anyone escaping during the time I was there but would have guessed that they would have to contact local authorities and report us missing to them. For that reason, we need to stay off of main roads and highways. But we also needed to get to the Upper Peninsula and certainly didn't want to walk the whole way. I really hoped we wouldn't have to.

We stayed in the woods as much as possible for the remainder of the walk that first day. We did manage to stay on the edge of the woods though so we could follow the road and see signs to help us know which direction we were heading, making sure it was north.

We also came across a sign that said "Welcome to Burton" which I guess solved the mystery to the city we were in. The sign faced the opposite way that we were going so, I guessed we were now leaving Burton, Michigan. Right before dark we came across a rest stop, a pretty large one sitting off the roadway on top of a hill.

"I do believe we have found our accommodations for the night kids." Isaac stated.

"This will be perfect." Kora chimed in.

There weren't any cars in the parking spots around the building. We made our way inside and the first thing we did was hit the vending machines inside, spending the first of our stolen money. I was really cold and really hungry, I assumed the same for Kora and Isaac. We took our treats and drinks and went into the cleaning closet room that wasn't locked but actually left ajar. Thank you cleaning man, I thought to myself. This was so much better than the cold night air that was getting colder by the minute.

Our journey continued in the same fashion for the next three days and nights. Always making sure we had a rest stop to camp in at night. We could warm up and get food to replenish us. Granted, it was mostly junk food, but it was cheap and making our money go a lot farther than if we were trying to eat in restaurants. And traveling this way kept us out of site. We had made it to a city called Gaylord.

According to the maps in the rest stops we were heading in the right direction and we were not too far from the Upper Peninsula.

In a rest stop in Gaylord, Michigan, we had settled into a far corner wall to try and get some rest, not all of the janitors, or whatever you called the people who cleaned these places, would leave the cleaning closet door unlocked. In fact, the majority did not, forcing us to rest right out in the open. We would try and be as out of site as one could be in a building like that. It must have been midnight when we settled into that far corner wall. There usually wasn't very many people coming or going by that time of night. On this night, right after we had gotten comfortable, a young man walked in. He didn't notice us right away but as he got closer he most certainly did. It looked as though he was taken aback by us, I could imagine he was, here were three people dressed in all white huddled against the corner wall of the rest stop. He looked us over and then gave a smile and continued making his way to the men's bathroom. We gave each other the same look we did every time someone had come in after we had settled in and noticed us. The reaction we got from them once exiting the facility would help us decide whether we could stay or should leave. It wasn't long and the man was walking out of the hall leading from the men's bathroom. He looked at us again, raised his eyebrows a little and kept walking.

Kora whipped her head toward us and informed us we could not stay. In fact, she thought we needed to leave immediately. I agreed with her, that man was very suspicious of us. As much as I did not want to sleep outside it was better than the alternative, being caught and sent back to hell. We all jumped up and headed for the side door we had just entered not long ago. Isaac opened the door and Kora went to go through first, almost running right into the man coming back in as we were making our hasty exit. All of us froze. The man gave an honest smile and then spoke. "Hey. Um, look I am not interested in causing any trouble for you guys at all, I swear. You look nervous so I just wanted you to know that. My name is Jackson and I was just wondering if you wanted a ride somewhere or something. It looks like you could use some help and I have room in my van. I am heading back to Paradise which is like a few hours from here so if you were heading that way it wouldn't be a problem to drop you anywhere along that route." After a short, awkward moment of silence, Isaac asked where Paradise was. When the man told us it was in the Upper Peninsula our eyes got big I'm sure. I felt like we could trust this guy for some reason. After being around so many heartless people it seemed as though I had developed a better sense to gage if someone was trustworthy or not. Then, after a very short, private conversation amongst just Kora, Isaac and I we found ourselves heading toward this man's van.

Paradise

I loved the town we ended up in called Paradise, it felt like Paradise. I guess keeping in mind where we had just come from any place may have been amazing, but it truly is a very picturesque place. The time I spent at the hospital seemed to erase so many good memories I may have had from my past. I am so grateful that Jackson came into that rest stop, on that night, at that exact time that he did. And since that night he had welcomed Kora, Isaac and I into his small rental home. Jackson had been our savior.

The three of us, since arriving, have applied and been accepted at a community college less than thirty minutes away. And all three of us have found part time jobs in the community. Jackson wasn't any different, he was working and finishing his schooling. He was way ahead of us with his schooling, he already has his associate's degree and was finishing his bachelor's degree online while working full time at a local bank as a loan officer. Life really seemed to be as it should be.

There was lots to do in Paradise, if you enjoy the great outdoors. One of our favorite things is to rent kayaks and go along the pictured rock shoreline. There are some amazing water caves that you can actually paddle your kayak right into. There are also spots along the shore to climb up onto the edge of the rock, you can lay out in the sun or jump off and swim. We always brought drinks and food so we could spend the whole day. Eventually, instead of continuously renting, we all purchased our own kayaks. Isaac and I also really enjoyed hiking as another favorite thing to do, more so than the others. There were some really nice scenic trails right around us. Paradise was a great place to live.

There was something else to be excited about. I had finally gotten in touch with my cousin Sophie. It was a weird thing that happened. After turning eighteen, I felt comfortable getting my identifications back; my driver's license, a mailing address, library card and those kind of things that people have.

I was nervous about doing this initially but all of us sitting around one night discussed the risk in getting those things back. Jackson made the point that when we were put in the hospital we were minor's and it was not because of a criminal offense but rather because of mental state issues, caused by a horrific event. We all agreed that we had to take the chance to obtain these things once we were considered legal adults if we ever wanted to try and have any sort of normalcy. I just happened to have that happen, become an adult, a short time before Isaac or Kora. Not long after I took the step and applied for those things, I received a letter from my cousin Sophie. Thanks to an older nurse that worked at the hospital, who had a kind soul. She gave me the address she found for Sophie, which I had memorized, and it turned out to be right. I finally wrote her from outside of the crazy walls and not long after I sent it, I received a letter in return, that then turned into phone calls which then turned into her coming to visit.

Sophie arrived in Paradise mid-summer. This was the second time she had come to visit, but this time she doesn't leave. Sophie is a photographer, who worked for herself which made it easy for her to relocate so quickly and without much thought. She does private sessions for families or anyone who wants to hire her service but also does photography of the beautiful landscape around the area and sells lots of that work online.

Honestly, Sophie takes pictures of just about anything and everything, nothing was off limits.

Sophie did not have any answers for me regarding why I never had a visit or heard from any of my family. She said after the incident with my grandfather the whole family fell apart. My parents moved, she didn't know where or if they had stayed together. Sophie said she had made several calls to St. Jude to try and schedule a visit to come and see me but was told that I was in a persistent vegetative state and that it would only upset me if I had any kind of contact with a person from my past. Sophie of course did not want to bring me any more pain. Her father passed away during my absence and she wasn't sure about her mother. She hadn't been to the hospital to visit for some time, but she did say at her last visit her mother's health was declining. But the both of us were so happy to be reconnected and in the way we were able to, had to be fate.

The small rental house we all shared was a three bedroom, just a block away from Lake Superior. There is much love for that great lake. Lots of hours spent on the lakeshore, out in the water in the old boat Jackson had. Everyone does their part contributing to the house fund. Isaac, Sophie, Kora, me and Jackson all put in so much money every month to go toward the rent and utilities.

It worked out great with four of us, our money went a long ways. The girls all shared a large, oversized bedroom and Jackson and Isaac had their own pretty small ones.

Just like in the hospital, although on a much happier scale, here in Paradise, days turn into weeks and weeks into months and so on. Before long, and without recognizing the time it had been five years since the day we got into that van with Jackson. Everyone had grown into an adult job, each very different. Kora had bought a very cute little bungalow style house by the beach not far from the house we all shared and was a nurse at the hospital. I had found a lovely town house on the other side of town and was working for family services department as a social worker. Not as close to the beach as I was but no matter where you lived in this town, you weren't more than three minutes from the water. Isaac ended up buying and running a restaurant downtown. It had living quarters above that he lived in. And finally, the inevitable,

Sophie and Jackson, both working at the bank, found that they would probably want to live together till death do us part. Yes, we were planning a wedding.

Sophie and Jackson both agreed they wanted an outdoor wedding, on the beach, no surprise. It was going to be a simple wedding but still took an entire year for us to make sure we had every detail covered.

Sophie wanted the flowers on the tables to be white crown-beard in mason jars with nautical rope wrapped around the top of each jar. In the middle of the crown-beard was one single light pink rose. Sophie's bouquet was a beautiful arrangement of the same. The tables were set around in the sand and people could just sit at their table to watch the ceremony. Sophie looked breathtaking. Her dress was simple with spaghetti straps, no embellishments at all and it looked gorgeous on her. Jackson was very handsome in his beach linen khaki pants, white shirt and flip flops. They choose a Hawaiian Luau menu of food for the reception part and even included some local dancers who had mastered the art of hula dancing to perform. It turned out perfectly, everything Sophie had wanted it to be.

As for the rest of us, there was the occasional boyfriend or girlfriend, never turned into anything serious and always came to an end. And as far as Isaac and I or Isaac and Kora, we were too much like brothers and sisters to think of each other in any other way.

All five of us were living what seemed to be pretty happy, normal lives on the outside. We did have joy in our lives and happy times and moments. But we had scars. Big enough that we noticed. Scars that made sure we never quite felt like whole people, a bit broken. I had found working as a social worker was good for me in some ways and also painful.

I had great council for others but never could get it to work just right on myself. Although, who knows what kind of mess I may have been if it weren't for my knowledge of how to deal with the human psyche. Kora would say the same, the fact that she was a nurse helping others had helped her in so many ways but not enough to take away the pain completely.

Isaac seemed to let his anger loose more often than the rest of us. There were occasions at a local bar that he would take a disagreement with another patron too far. I believed the fact that he didn't share his past, what he had went through, like the rest of us, had a lot to do with that. As hard as it was to talk about, it did help in releasing some of the frustration and anger due to the inability to change something that you wish you could. It could lead to cynicism, discouragement, hopelessness and a variety of other unhelpful emotions.

The empty feeling I carried grew stronger as the years passed. I stayed busy with work and my friends, taking time to enjoy things I liked and yet at the end of each and every day there was still something missing inside. Kora and I would talk the most it seemed about that feeling we shared. But one Saturday afternoon as Isaac was over waiting for me to get ready to go on a hike he started to share, he started talking about the creation of his scar, his childhood, which ended him in the same hospital I ended up at. He started to share the things he had never spoke of before, other than in very small bits and pieces.

Isaac's Story

It was in an overcrowded trailer park in Detroit Michigan where Isaac's life began. Isaac was born into poverty with an out of work father, an overworked mother and one older sister. His mother worked as a housekeeper at one of the local motels. It was the kind of hotel that charged by the hour. His mother would go into work at three in the afternoon and not get home until after midnight. When school was going, Isaac and his sister didn't see much of their mother.

Most days went pretty much the same. The house awoke to yelling and fighting, coming from Isaac's parents. It usually started from the time his mother woke. It was always the same fight, about money. There wasn't enough of it. There could have been more if his father would get a job, a real job like his mother would say, that actually helped pay a bill, but instead he always had impossible dreams or get rich schemes that would almost always make things even worse. He also enjoyed gambling, he would tell Isaac and his sister that one day he was going to strike it rich. They wanted to believe him, they would get excited when they sat and listened to him talk about a new money making idea he had. Their mother never believed him and she no longer listened.

Isaac continued…

One day my father had an idea that mother initially dismissed like she always did. But after listening to him talk, very animated to me and my sister, she began to listen. My mom was in the kitchen washing dishes. We were in the living room that adjoined with the kitchen.

"There will be lots of other children to play with." Father exclaimed. He always made these new ventures sound amazing. "The best part of this would be that your mother would get to be at home with you guys. She wouldn't have to work like she does now, to the point where she is so tired she can't even enjoy her family. Wouldn't that be great? And dad would get to go to work, to do hard work.

We would grow our own food, live in a house that has fields to play in that are bigger than any yard you ever saw. And another thing is, no bad people. That's right, bad people do not get to live in this place." Mother had set her dish towel down and came and sat on the edge of the couch by us. The trailer park we lived in had plenty of bad people living in it.

"So what is this?" Mother asked. "What are you scheming up now Roger?"

"This isn't a scam, I swear. This would be a change of life for us! I have been looking into this for a long time now, wanting to make sure it is legit and all that. It is! It's a group of people, they call themselves "The Remnants".

"What does that mean?" My mother asked

"From what I have learned during conversations with some of the other members is that it is a group of people that have figured out a lot of the bullshit we are fed on a daily basis, is just that…bullshit. The way we struggle just to survive, fight with each other like we are in a civil war in this country. I am so sick of all the nonsense. I am sick of wondering if my family will be able to eat or be warm or have a pair of shoes to wear. This place would take away all of our worries. We would always have everything we needed. They believe in family. In the old ways of hard work and being there to raise your children. Neighbors helping neighbors. Being a community together."

"And how does that work?" Mother wanted to know.

"When you join them, you make a promise to them and they make a promise to you. They promise to always be there for you in every way needed.

Our promise to the group is pretty much the same. We will be part of the family, a community of people like us. There are rules and laws to obey to make sure the community stays safe and works like it is intended to. And like any good family, we will take care of and look out for each other. Live together, eat together, work and play together."

"So where does the money come from? Where would we live?" Mother was getting more curious about this newest plan.

"The men farm and do other odd jobs in the community. The woman take care of the children, the cooking, cleaning and also some money making things such as having bake sales, knitting blankets to sell, quilting, and the biggest money maker is their jams. The community has fields of strawberries that get picked and made into homemade jam that is put in individual jars and sold right off the side of the road. Cars line up to buy this jam I have been told. All money goes into a community fund and then it is decided by the family leaders how it will be dispersed.

Mother got up from the couch and walked back into the kitchen. She stood with her back to us with her hands on her hips for quite some time. I could tell she was deep in thought.

I don't remember exactly how long, but it wasn't more than a couple of weeks and we were packed and ready to go in our very old suburban heading to our new home somewhere in Kentucky.

Initially, it was great. The entire place was fenced in. We were told this was for our safety, father told us that is how they kept the bad people out. We got to live in a house in the far back part of the fenced in community. It was an old farm house but very clean and well maintained according to mother and father. There was a distressed white decorative fence along the sides and back of the house. There were also huge trees all around, they looked like great climbing trees to me. My sister and I went to school in the middle of the settlement in a small building. All of the kids went to school there no matter their age. We learned different things depending on how old you were, but I didn't always like being in school all day with my sister, she watched me like a hawk. I know she just wanted to look out for me but I got annoyed at times. And sometimes the older kids were mean.

Mother loved the community at first. She would hum as she moved around the house. Sometimes she would even laugh which we hardly ever heard coming from her. It was a nice sound. One of the rules here was that woman had to wear dresses, even the girls.

My sister complained for a while but then I guess she must have gotten used to it. The boys & men had to wear dark pants and button up cotton shirts. There were dress ones and work ones.

All of the children had school from eight in the morning until one in the afternoon. The rest of their day on weekdays were spent doing chores until dinner time. The days were long and sometimes hard. But not as hard, or as bad, as when we were in our small trailer where sometimes we didn't have lights, water or food because we couldn't pay for them. We always had those things here, just like father had promised. But, it didn't take long before this promised- land turned into an unpleasant experience filled with agony.

One of the memories I still have nightmares about is a game that I was forced to play with some of the other children. Forced by means of peer pressure I should say. They called it 'Bath Time'. According to the other children I was playing with, they had all played before, so now I had to take a turn and then I could belong to their group. The game sounded scary but I agreed to play along. I told myself it was just a game, that it wasn't real. The rules were that you had to use a cloth baby doll, cut it open and remove the filling, then refill it with oatmeal. Supposedly the oatmeal would absorb a spirit into the doll like it absorbs water when you cook it.

After doing that the person playing had to sew the doll up and lay her in whatever room you wanted the spirit to be in. Then wait six hours, six minutes and six seconds before checking on it. If the spirit was satisfied then it would stay where it was set, but it would no longer be facing the direction you had set it. If the doll was not where you set it, and was somewhere else in the house, it meant you had gotten a bad entity. Whatever had entered the doll was not good or satisfied, and was letting you know it was not going to be contained.

If the doll was not where you left it there was also another possibility. The evil spirit was lying in wait for the player of the game. The doll had been moved but the evil returned to the original spot to hold-up until the person returned. Then it could possess the person. My friend Sarah at the time tried to calm my nerves about playing.

"That has never happened Isaac." Sarah tried to reassure me.

"Actually, it has." Timmy told her. "Remember Mr. Swanson? He found out that his daughter had played 'Bath Time' and she claimed that weird things started happening to her afterward. He wanted to prove to her that none of it was real. So he played, right after he began to act strangely. I heard my parents talking to Mr. and Mrs. Dwight about it last year. People said he was behaving like he was possessed.

They would see him crawling on his hands and legs around his yard like a dog. Then, on Halloween night that same year, his daughter killed him! She said he was trying to hurt her. She killed him with his own axe in their barn. No one knows for sure what happened at their place that night. Some people said it was actually the daughter who had been possessed and was like a witch, making her father do strange things."

"Maybe we should play Monopoly or something instead." I tried joking but was entirely serious.

"Come on, let's do this!" Timmy yelled and took off running in the direction of my house.

I did all of the preparations with the doll since it was 'my turn'. I also had no choice where we played, the game was to be played at my house, another rule. I choose the basement as the room I would put her. I figured that would be the best place since I never went down there. If a spirit did attach itself, it could stay down there!

We had taken the doll from the school, out of the kindergarten area. A little girl seen us walking out of the building with it and started crying, telling us to bring Sophia back. We ignored her and made our way to my house where I began to prepare for the game. It felt odd cutting this doll open, almost as though I had begun this sinful journey that I wasn't able to turn back from.

Nobody was home at my house. Dad was working and mother had went to the nearest town to get some staple items that we weren't able to provide for ourselves with one of the neighbor ladies. The house seemed eerily quiet, although I'm sure that's just because I was nervous and afraid of what I had to do. I had placed her in a corner in the basement facing the wall. After completing all the requirements of the game we all went outside to wait. One of the boys set an alarm for six hours, six minutes and six seconds from the moment I had set the doll down. It would be in between lunch and supper when it would be time to check on the doll.

All of us went to the back of the property, there was this really high rock wall. We loved playing there and pretending we were climbing mountains. Today was filled with a bit more impatience than usual. Our thoughts weren't exactly on climbing Mt. Everest or whatever name we had given it on that day. I had sat on a rock half way up and looked around at the area I lived in. I looked around at the lush, green flat fields that led into some rolling hills and thought to myself how much I would love to run across all of it and just continue running. I often had feelings like that, wanting to run away. "Isaac!" One of the girls in the group was yelling. She was standing on the ground looking up at me. "It's lunch time." Then I heard it. The lunch bell, ringing loudly, over and over again. The rest of the group I was with were already running back toward the dining hall.

I climbed down and walked back with Sarah. "Are you afraid?" She asked. "Sort of." I lied. I was terrified.

"I am too." She said and gave me a kind look, then ran off ahead of me.

After lunch we went to the large communal garden and started weeding. We picked some carrots that were ready and delivered them to Mrs. Blitho in the kitchen area of the dining hall. Mrs. Blitho asked that we go and pick two bushels of apples for her to make desserts for the next day. After picking and delivering the apples we decided to return to the rock wall to wait out the remainder of the time, which wasn't much.

Walking back to my house was nerve racking. I was trying to convince myself to not freak out no matter what. We entered through the back door and moved slowly to the basement door. As we walked down the stairs there was a sudden rush of cool air that passed by all of us. Everyone turned and looked back up the stairs in the direction the blast of cold was heading. "What was that?" Sarah whispered.

"Nothing. Let's go." I answered. I continued down the stairs and around the corner. My eyes staring straight ahead, piercing the wall that separated us from the doll on the other side. I moved over with my next step and hugged the plastered wall, placing my hand on it and took the final turn around the corner.

The other kids made their way past me and stood off to the side a bit. My eyes became as big as saucers as I looked at the empty corner. The doll was not there. "Oh no." Someone said, I couldn't tell who.

Timmy turned his head around and stared at me with eyes wide open. "Run!" he yelled

I ran up the stairs, through the house and out the front door. I ran around to the back of the house and through the yard to the barn. Then I ran into the barn with my legs still going as fast as they could go. Once inside, I didn't waste any time looking for a place to hide. I immediately headed to the bales of hay stacked as high as the top of the barn itself. The bales were square so I was able to run up them quickly. When I reached the top, I carefully slid my legs over to the back side of the bales and tucked my head down so I would not be noticed.

I stayed there without moving for a long time. Then I could hear the kids that I played the game with, or I should say that had watched me play. They were at the door of the barn talking and yelling for me. I didn't answer at first but then raised myself up high enough so they could see me. "What the hell!" Timmy hollered.

"You tell me!" I hollered back

"Come on. We are supposed to be helping serve dinner tonight. We are going to be late because of you." He was trying to act angry but I could tell he was freaked out.

"Where is the doll?" I asked.

"We didn't see it. Doesn't matter. The whole thing was a joke anyway. It's not real stupid! Your mom must have seen it down there and taken it." Timmy wasn't looking at me when he was telling me this. He was looking at the ground and shifting from one leg to the other.

"Cool game." I said sarcastically.

I didn't believe him about it not being real, or maybe I did. I didn't know what to think. Weeks later I did find out that Timmy was right about one thing. My mother had seen the doll and moved it. She couldn't figure out where it came from but didn't like the looks of it. I don't recall what she said she did with it.

The one thing I was beginning to realize was that the community was beginning to stink. And not just because they played stupid games, there were other things that were bad.

My father started to change. He was not acting like his usual fun loving, positive thinking, everything is going to be ok self. He seemed angry a lot and lost his temper pretty regularly. On the other hand, mother seemed to get happier by the day and didn't seem to be bothered by my father's anguish at all. They hardly ever fought anymore, in fact, they barely talked. She did talk a lot to our closest neighbor John though. John's wife had passed away a year prior from cancer I believe.

He never came to visit when my father was home which I didn't think much about at the time. Sometimes I would see him and mother walking along the tree line in the backyard. They were always smiling and laughing. Mother had a different kind of life in the community. She still worked very hard, but no longer had the stresses that existed daily back in Detroit. I remember feeling happy for her.

At this point, my sister Michelle and I were no longer enjoying the community life we were living. We didn't have the freedoms that many kids our age did. We ate at the same times every day, with the same group of people. Sometimes it would have been nice to eat at our house, with just us. We went to bed at the same time every night, even on the weekends. We had to wear different clothes than we used to. There were lots of rules that we questioned but were not allowed to question. I guessed lots of kids felt that way but our way of life was becoming more and more difficult to live for me. I was beginning to feel suffocated. I never got to meet anyone outside of the community. I felt like I didn't matter, that only the entire group mattered.

And then there was the issue with a group of older boys. Sometimes this group would take me behind the school during a morning recess and beat me with a whip, or with wooden sticks. The teacher hardly ever came out to watch us, she was always busy preparing for the afternoon.

One boy would take a few swings and then give it to his buddy to do the same. It was very painful. They were careful not to hit me in the face, and then also warned me every time about what would happen if I told anyone about these beatings. Once in a while they would grab one of the other smaller boys to beat on.

One day they grabbed a boy named Tommy. The biggest boy in the group had struck him in the leg first with the whip and I could see the blood start to come through his pant leg. The boy was holding Tommy's face on the ground in the dirt and I could see the tears start rolling down his cheek. I don't recall thinking about intervening but that is exactly what happened. I jumped on the back of this large boy and started hitting him in the back of his head as hard as I could. The other kids standing around started cheering for me. It made me feel great. But it didn't last long before one of the other boys in the group grabbed me and threw me to the ground. On this day I felt different. I had had enough. I was twelve years old and I knew I had to fight back, which is exactly what I did. I started kicking and yelling at them, swinging my arms wildly trying to keep them away. I remember them laughing. Then one of the boys tackled me from behind. After that, the fight was over, for me anyway. The beating on that day was really bad. I felt the whip lashing across my back. One boy was pushing my head into the dirt ground and one was sitting on my feet.

They would always chant, "Beat the nasty city out of him! You think your tough boy!" And other ridiculous things like that. I stopped trying to get up, I turned my head and seen my sister standing with some of the other kids. There were tears streaming down her face. The boy with the whip stood up and looked around at the group of children witnessing the event and reminded them that they were not to say a word about this. My eyes met with my sister's and we stared at each other for a few seconds, then she turned and ran away. I never told…my sister did.

The next thing I remembered was the teacher yelling. "Get off of him! Stop it right now!" One last hit with the whip, and it landed right on the side of my face. It hurt so bad my entire body reacted, I ended up in a fetal position lying face down. The teacher and some of the students rushed over to help me and were trying to get me up. I was brought to the family medical leader's house. She cleaned me up and reassured me that I would heal, but the lashing on my face may scar.

When I arrived home that day both my mother and father were there waiting. They came running up to me and hugged me. They were both so sorry about what had happened and promised it would never happen again. For a long time after that day my mother would walk to the school every day at our recess time to sit and watch.

My sister loved it, I felt more awkward and unwelcomed from the other kids. In fact, I never really felt like I fit in with the other kids at this place. The boys who had done the beating had to work in the gardens for a month as punishment. No school, just pulling weeds and picking strawberries.

One Sunday after church there was a communal picnic. The family leaders had their lengthy table set up outside. My father asked a family member what was going on and the man said there was going to be some kind of announcement. Some of the older kids started a game of baseball, others were playing duck, duck goose and the smaller children were singing and dancing to ring around the rosie, which always gave me the creeps. The adults were standing and sitting around in groups visiting. Some of the men were grilling, hot dogs and hamburgers. The woman had made salads and desserts.

After some time the eldest family leader blew his whistle, which meant for everyone to stop and to be quiet because he was going to speak to everyone as a group. He started out with a friendly greeting, "Good afternoon family." Which everyone replied to with a good afternoon. "I have some exciting news. The other family leaders and I have been discussing a great opportunity for us, for all of us. My dream has always been to grow, in size, we want to be a family that has branches all over this fine country and the way to do that is to spread our seeds in different places.

We feel that a good way to help more people is to branch out. After much discussion over many a night we have come to a decision on what three internal families we would like to leave here and start a new community somewhere else. Working together to find good people to join our family. Teach them our way of life, expand and make as many good people as possible want to be part of 'The Remnants'. It is with great honor I stand before you all and give you the name of the first group chosen. Then he announced, "Roger Kaster, his wife and their two children!" There was huge applause. I looked over at my mother and noticed that she looked confused, her eyes were staring straight ahead and not blinking, her face turned white, almost as if someone had taken her breath away. She looked at my father and was shaking her head no. He told her they would talk about it later. I noticed my mother scanning around with her eyes. She looks terrified. Then the other two groups are announced, there is a standing ovation for all of us. My father was smiling like he had not in quite some time.

We stayed for a few more weeks and then loaded up the very old suburban again and headed west. To California. The other two groups left at the same time. I'm assuming my parents had been told where to go in California to set up a new community. It took about a week to get where we were going to settle. The ride was long but we took lots of stops which helped. The women had packed coolers with lunch meats, breads and other foods to eat along the way.

We ended up in a place known as The Shasta Cascade Region in a city by the name of Faction. It was breathtaking. Absolutely beautiful. A small town with friendly people. Of course we weren't going to be neighbors with any of them because the piece of property that the Remnants were going to live on was all by itself way out in the middle of nowhere. It was a beautiful nowhere but still had no one and nothing civilized around.

We had enough money to start building some structures for living in right away. But in the meantime, it was tent city. The tents consisted of large, heavy tarps we had brought with us that ended up being used to form what looked like teepees. Those were pretty much used for sleeping. In addition to that we had a large tarp that was stretched out and tied with rope on top of some trees that worked as posts. This was our open kitchen area. Used for cooking, eating, meeting and any other times the whole group needed to gather. The men built picnic tables for sitting and shelves for setting dishware and food on. That is how things started.

We had been in the area for months before we added anyone to the family. It was a single man. He came walking up over the hill one day and didn't leave. He said he was walking across the country trying to find somewhere to call home. As soon as he seen our tents and the beginning of some real structures being built, he said he knew he had found it.

The area we were in he referred to as 'unspoiled'. We had lakes and rivers, mountains and waterfalls, hills and valleys. The man's name was Jim and he was a giant of a man. He must have been all of six foot five inches tall, towering over everyone else, and came across as a gentle, kind person. Jim didn't spend much time talking about himself or telling us anything too personal. He looked to be in his thirties and said he did not have a wife or any children. My father said he was a fine addition to the family. He was always helping everyone with anything they needed help with. I had never seen him angry or upset and we worked together almost every day. I was learning how to do carpentry work with him and a couple of the other men. There were five homes being constructed at the same time. At that time, the shell of each was about complete. We had two outhouses and didn't have plans for indoor plumbing any time soon. Cleaning up was done in the river that was not far from camp. That included cleaning of ourselves and hauling water back for dishes or whatever else it was needed for. For instance, we boiled it for drinking and cooking.

One day, after I was done working on one of the houses, my sister and I decided we were going to go down to the river to relax and swim. It was a very hot summer day. I think it was a Saturday, although sometimes I didn't know what day it was. It wasn't like we had a school schedule or anything like that so I would forget sometimes.

My sister and I had a connection where we could almost tell what each other was thinking without speaking. We began to walk toward the water, I looked over and she had this smirk on her face, her eyebrows above her big round brown eyes were raised. I knew immediately what that meant. It was going to be a race to the water! The two of us took off running full speed, I thought about tripping her which would have worked but we were running so fast I thought she might get hurt, so I didn't. What I did do was run in her direction to get in front of her so she had to slow down. She squealed and pushed me. We were both laughing by this time and slowing our pace to what was more of a fast skipping motion.

Jim was at the river when we got there. He was just sitting with his feet dangling in the water. He signaled for us to join him when he noticed us. "How are you two doing today?" Jim asked

"Not too bad. But it's so hot here." My sister, Michelle answered.

"Let's go for a swim. That will surely cool us down." Jim stood up and grabbed my sister by the hand and led her into the water. The sight of my fifteen year old sister who was quite small walking next to Jim who was so huge looked really bizarre. I joined them for a little while. We all would lay on our backs and let the current take us downstream, then turn over on our stomach and swim back. The water felt great in the hot sun. Jim stood up at one point, letting the current move around his thighs like he was standing in still water.

He looked me right in the eye and said, "Ya know Isaac, life may not be the party we hoped for, but we should take it all in and enjoy. You know what I mean?" I nodded my head, I understood what he meant and agreed. He said things like that often. Eventually I got out of the water and yelled that I was going to go and get us a snack and would be right back. Jim was standing in the water letting my sister stand on his hands that were cupped together, then he would throw her into the deep water over his shoulder. She would scream and laugh at the same time. It made me happy to see her having fun. She looked over at me and waved to let me know she heard me. I gave a wave back, turned and ran back to the camp. That was the last time I saw my sister…alive. It was also the last time anyone saw Jim.

The family searched for Michelle for a little more than a week. Along the river and in the woods, for miles in all directions. When they gave up and stopped looking, I continued. Any free time I had, I would search. I would sneak out at night and search. I never found anything. Nothing that would even insinuate that she was ever there. The loss of my sister did a lot of damage. I was devastated, my father began staying away from home as much as possible and my mother checked out for the most part. I was sitting at the table eating breakfast one morning when my father walked by me, grabbed his keys off of the counter and walked out the door to go to work like any other day.

Except he no longer would speak, would not say good-bye, and would not smile. I realized at that moment that things would never be the same. I think that even though everyone knew deep down inside we would probably never see Michelle again, there wasn't that feeling of closure because we didn't know for sure.

The entire family understandably became very weary of strangers which made it difficult to try and grow and let new people in. Ultimately, it was felt that the settlement in California was not going to survive. The family had grown to twenty three since arriving, including the three families that started the community, and not one new addition since the disappearance of Michelle.

The community in the Shasta Cascade Region loved where they were and didn't want to leave. The family leaders met and came to the conclusion that the family could stay for a time, but at the years end they would meet and see if it had become any more prosperous and then go from there on whether or not to keep this community where it was.

So once again my father and a couple of other families were asked to move and start a new community in Oklahoma this time. The family leaders wanted something already in place in case they needed to move the California community.

I was allowed to stay in California for another month and then could ride out with another family that was leaving later.

I had one month left to find my sister. My buddy Kevin would come with me and help most days. On one of those days we walked quite a ways into the woods following the creek that flowed into the river. It would be nothing but a trickle in some areas and then fast moving bubbling water in others. We had planned on hiking quite a distance that day so we packed a lunch and brought drinks with us. Kevin was walking on the opposite side from me, both of us scanning the ground around us as we walked. I yelled across to ask him if he wanted to stop now and take a break to eat our lunch. He didn't respond so I turned to see if he heard me. He was standing completely still in one spot and was staring down at the ground. I yelled his name twice before he looked up at me. "What did you find?" I hollered. He just stared at me but wouldn't answer. Frustrated and nervous at the same time, I stomped through the creek to get over to where Kevin was standing, I walked over and stood next to him. He continued to look at me with this look of sympathy on his face. I suddenly felt enraged. I tried to ignore his eyes on me and looked down at the spot he had been gazing at. Then I saw what made him stop and stare. It was pink with a white flower on the top.

I remember when Michelle bought those flip flops. We were in town, a rare thing for us to be able to go along, and she begged our mother for them. Finally mother gave in but was a dollar short. There was an older woman behind us in line that heard all of what was transpiring between the clerk and our mother and slid a dollar bill into my sister's hand to pay the difference. She looked at my sister and whispered, "Shoes are a lot like ice-cream honey, there's always room for more." Michelle smiled, laughed and thanked her. And now, here lie one of those shoes. It was really dirty, most of the white flower was covered with dried mud. All of the hope I had that my sister was still with us ended at that very moment. Kevin backed off and gave me some time to sit by myself in the spot the shoe lie in the dirt. I sat there and imagined the moment that she lost it, the struggle, how afraid she must have been. After some time of me basically mourning, Kevin agreed to continue the search, we were obviously in the right area now.

Her body was lying in the creek. Her hand extended onto the dry land as well as her right foot. She was face down in the water with a large log across her back. There was some green vegetation lying over part of her leg that had little white flowers on it. Her hair was flowing in the water with the current, repeating its course over and over again. She was so bloated, it didn't really look like her, but it was her. I noticed the other flip flop still partially on her foot, it had stayed hooked in her toes. She was wearing the angel wing necklace I had given her for her birthday. It was very dainty and had small diamond accents on the outside of the wings. It was twisted and laying on her shoulder, shimmering in the sun.

I can still hear my mother's screams from that day, when I told her that I had found Michelle. Her screams and the vision of the body lying bloated in the creek are almost always haunting some part of my day, every day.

Not very long after that, I left and joined my parents in Oklahoma. The family only allowed us to remain because they felt badly for us, we certainly were not behaving like the family wants its members to any longer. I was never the same. There was so much anger in me and no one knew how to help. I helped myself…to drugs, alcohol and anything else that would help to erase that memory for any length of time. One night, just about a year before you got to St. Jude's I did some bath salt. I flipped out, went crazy and almost died. That is some nasty shit and I would not recommend it. It was a great excuse for my parent's to have me institutionalized. They weren't much better anyway. My mother was popping pills daily to masque her sorrow and my father was never around. Between the three of us, we never really saw each other, we were always heading in different directions running from the pain.

Waking Up

I feel very groggy trying to wake up. It takes a few minutes for me to recall where I am. I feel the sun shining through the roof. It feels like I have slept for weeks. So many dreams that were so real, recalling every moment leading up to right here and now. Not sure they should be defined as dreams. More like playing a movie that you had seen before, a true story you lived, and you are the star, reflecting on memories of years gone by.

Reality hits me so vividly. Everything is so very clear and I feel more awake than I ever have. I am on Ezra Island. Me, Isaac, Kora, Jackson and Sophie.

After hiking for days we have found the slides and have decided to climb them. I am back in the present.

I wonder if the dreams I had were like the picture show that apparently will play before us right before we die. I had never heard that this happens during the sleep state but reality seems to be not as real as it once was anyway. Reliving everyone's story was painful, I am still feeling stressed. And now that I am back in real time, the stress is getting worse.

The zip door of my tent is open. I can see the others moving about outside through the opening. I must be the last to wake. Then, a set of feet appear in front of the opening. "I know those feet." I say. Isaac's head pops into the opening with a big smile.

"Good morning princess. Why don't you get your happy ass up and join the festivities taking place on the other side of these nylon walls." Isaac raises his eyebrows in an amusing manner as he leaves the opening and stands up.

"Okay. Okay." I said. I wondered if anyone had changed their mind.

As I exited the tent I could see the mood of the others was pretty solemn. Judging by that I made the assumption we were going through with the plan. The conversation stayed mainly about what to do with our gear, we decided to leave it but we did layer our clothes.

Everything got packed up and set together under a tree.

I sit down in the middle of the slides and stare at them all. My thought is, maybe one will call to me.

Isaac starts to say something but Sophie suddenly stands, walks away from us and looks toward the sky. Jackson shifts to get up. I place my hand on his shoulder. "Give her a minute." I tell him. He remains sitting but with a watchful eye on her. Sophie turns back toward us and looks over each of us.

"Why is it not one of you has asked me about my days at the hospital?'

"Sophie?" I ask, letting her know I didn't understand the question.

"All those visits to see my mother. All those years. All those weekends wasted and lost to visiting a place that still presents me with such vivid dreams I rely on prescription sleeping pills to try and allow myself the rest I deserve."

I try to answer the best I can. "I feel like we have been there for you. You have shared some with me about those years. I have not questioned or pushed anyone else to share more than they have. I think when someone goes through something horrible they should be allowed to heal and deal how they need to."

Sophie lowers her eyes toward the ground. "Yeah. You're right but just because mine might not seem as tragic as what you guys have went through doesn't mean it didn't impact my life. I hated when the weekend would come. Dreaded walking the long sidewalks that led to the oversized building that housed my mother. And then there was the other patients, always trying to touch me. The old women stroking my hair, walking around with their baby dolls as though they were real babies. The worst thing was my mother's eyes. Always pleading with me as she sat there not saying a word. That was even worse than the creepy janitor that always wanted me to go with him to get a bowl of ice-cream or some other kind of treat." She looked at Jackson for a moment and then continued.

"I feel the same as the rest of you. I feel an emptiness too. Something has always been missing for me. I grew up with looks of sympathy from everyone who was aware of my mother who talked to the dead. Kind of like yours Kora but they gave mine a different name...schizophrenic. And you Jackson...the night terrors you suffer with. Why is it we don't know your whole story. We should all be in the know before the climb. What if we need to know so we are aware once we get to whatever lies beneath? Know what we are looking for? Know who we need to help?"

"Well, you certainly have made broken look beautiful." Jackson says to Sophie. He clears his throat quite loudly. He looks a bit nervous as he begins to talk, "Your right Sophie. I agree. I would like to take the time to share with you all.

I know so much about all of your pasts, your ghosts that haunt you and I have not shared mine. I realize this has turned from being the white elephant in the room in the beginning to becoming our normal. But before we take this journey, I will share my story." He extends his hand for Sophie to join us again.

The Bayou

"I could hear the music in the distance. I was fourteen at the time. I recall the night air smelling of smoke. Mist was coming off of the swamp in a graceful manner. It was a special night I had been told. On that night my father would be inducted into Papa Joseph's special group. I didn't fully understand what his special group was, what I did realize, was how excited my father was."

Jackson was sitting next to me but his eyes focused off in the distance and he continued to tell us his story.

"The excitement had started a few weeks prior. My father and I lived on the outskirts of Lafayette, Louisiana.

There was a network of people that lived basically in the swamps, and we were one of them. We had our own laws, leaders, celebrations and that sort of thing. Our own community. Probably quite similar to you Isaac. Nobody was allowed to go into the city without permission. This was how I grew up, for the first fourteen years anyway. Apparently, my mother and father had lived in the city when I was born. My mother died from complications giving birth to me. Not long after, my father quit his job and moved us to the swamp. Disconnected from family and friends."

It appeared as though Jackson was reliving the memories as he spoke. He started telling us as far back as he could remember. He started talking of times when he was probably five or six he thought. Some of these early memories were a bit foggy. Perceptions may not be as accurate as the ones from when he got older.

Jackson's earliest memory is running down a hill and losing his footing because his legs started going faster than he could keep up. He said he tumbled and rolled until he came to a stop. He stayed on the ground, laying on his back and noticed this huge wooden figure towering up toward the sky almost right in front of him. He could not remember what it was, but thought it looked like a snake. The memory is short but strongly remembered. When he asked his father about it he was told it helped keep un-welcomed spirits out.

He also spoke of the big hall where the families would often get together. The building he recalls was like an open pavilion. There were many tables inside and just a roof over head with open walls to the outside. Kids would run in and out playing. In the center was a huge fire pit. I was very intrigued, Jackson had not shared like this. He continued...

The rougarou was a favorite story the parents used to tell us kids, to keep us near. The swamp lands were vast. They would warn us children that if we wondered too far away, the rougarou, which was supposedly like a werewolf, would smell us and hunt us down. They described the animal as being as tall as the tallest dog we had ever seen with claws longer than their feet. It could be any color but was usually white. The ones that appeared a color other than white meant that they were not pure rougarou. They were half breeds. If half was a tame dog that could mean you might have a slight chance of escaping if you encountered this beast. But, if the half was another form of wild dog than your chance of survival would be less than zero. We were told their hair stood up on the back of their neck and hung long below the belly. In any case, we did not want to run into any of these creatures. The scare tactic worked well, the children stayed close.

When I was around nine years old there was a picnic that happened on a hot summer day where all the families gathered at the big hall.

The kids were all eating watermelon and running around playing tag. A little girl probably the same age tagged me and I immediately took chase back after her. She was quite fast, zipping in and out of the tree lines. Then, she was gone. I couldn't see her anywhere. I stopped running and looked in all directions, but didn't see her. Then I realized how far I had gone into the woods. My heart sank and then began pounding. I swear you could have heard it, it felt like it was going to burst right out of my chest. I started yelling for my friend. She didn't answer. I panicked and started to run as fast as my legs could go. I didn't know if I was running in the direction that would bring me back to the community or deeper into the wooded swamp. I was looking all around as I was running, so worried the rougarou was chasing, and then I tripped over a fallen log. I landed right on my face. I picked my head up out of the wet ground and seen this mangy looking tail moving through the trees up ahead. It was as white as freshly fallen snow. My heart sank to the lowest pit in my stomach and I couldn't catch my breath. Then, there was a gunshot behind me. I whipped my head around and saw my dad running towards me. He was yelling for me to get up but before I could get to my knees he was at my side grabbing my arm and pulling me to my feet. He looked frantic, kept mumbling about me running off and that we had to get out of there. We ran all the way back to the big hall, well, my dad ran and pretty much drug me the whole way. I really don't know what I saw that day but it was a long time before I wondered away any distance again.

The people living in the swamps around us were very spiritual. They practiced what I believe was a form of hoodoo and other types of religion mixed with magic. There were often rituals held at the big hall, and other events held there as well. Some of the rituals were scary to me. I didn't always understand what was going on. There were free range chickens running around. Sometimes one of the chickens would be sacrificed. Sometimes for dinner, sometimes for their blood and sometimes, for both. Most of the houses were right on the water's edge. We didn't dare swim in the surrounding swamps because they were filled with gators. There was a group that kept watch of the property for any that wandered onto our land. They would make rounds every so often every day. If someone spotted a gator, we would let one of the members of this group know and they would deal with it. All of the men would hunt and kill the gators to sell. It was a small income that helped get supplies each family needed. The woman would make things out of the alligator heads and teeth, also they made things that were found in the earth surrounding the community. They would bring these items to market once a month and sell them. This also helped supplement income for supplies families needed. Sometimes the kids got to go into the city with the woman but not always. I think we were brought when times were tough, I'm sure when people from the city seen us children in our raggedy clothing and dirty faces they were sympathetic and would purchase things they didn't even want. Some people would holler river rats at us as they walked past. I didn't know what they meant by that. At times, people would come to the booth and put money in the cup the woman had set out for tips without buying anything. I could see the looks on their faces and it made me feel like I should be embarrassed.

That was the only time the children were allowed to go into the city. We didn't see Dr.'s, we had a medicine man. We didn't shop for barely any of our clothing at a store. A group of woman made clothing and some were handed down. The woman did go to thrift stores for certain things such as under garments and sometimes they would purchase other items depending on the price and what the money situation was at that shopping time. Mostly though they bought fabric and would sew the clothes. Our food was mostly hunted and the rest bought from local farmers not far from the swamps.

Anyway, back to when I was fourteen. It was a few weeks before my dad's big day. I woke up to a couple of my buddies throwing sticks at me threw my bedroom window. They were trying not to laugh but being very unsuccessful in their attempt. It was actually the laughing that woke me not the sticks. I threw my blanket over my head and waved my arms for them to go away. The sun was up but I wasn't ready to be. Then I heard my dad's voice inviting them into the house.

The next thing I knew I had about a hundred and twenty pounds crashing on my legs and another hundred and twenty pounds crashing on my upper body.

It was Jase and Toby, my best friends and partners in crime. We had a lot of fun running around in those swamps causing a little trouble here and there, when and if we could. And we were allowed to carry weapons such as knives at that point so we could protect ourselves if need be. But still were not allowed to wander alone. But on that day Jase and Toby wanted to go wrestle up a couple of gators. Toby's uncle would give us two dollars a foot. I was pretty sure we were getting ripped off but we didn't care. We always had fun catching them and it was a little spending money. Mostly used for chew and magazines. Toby's uncle would gather those items for us. He said young men require certain items the woman wouldn't shop for.

It was a warm July morning. I loved the summers in the swamp. The last day of school was a week ago today. We did not go to regular school in the city, we were homeschooled. All of the children congregated into one barn like building. It ran from November first through July first. We had two teachers, Mr. Sam and Ms. Melanie. School started at six in the morning Monday through Thursday. Friday's were lessons in the swamp with a couple of the elders. It was usually Mr. Griffin and Mr. Durand but sometimes others would fill in.

We learned all kinds of things. What poisonous snakes to watch for and what to do if we got bit. Learning the behavior of the alligators, how to avoid conflict if we ran into them. Basically, swamp survival 101.

I sat up on my bed, and took my time grabbing my pants and shirt from the end of the bed. Jase and Toby were impatiently pacing across my small bedroom floor. A very big part of our friendship was to irritate the shit out of each other. After a few more minutes of me delivering my slow getting around torture to them Toby grabbed my shirt out of my hands and put it on over my head then pushed me up off my bed.

The day started out good. We snagged two gators before lunch. Both of them sunning on the bank of the river. I had packed a few sandwiches for us before we left so we took the time to sit and eat. The conversation turned into the upcoming celebration for my dad. Both Toby and Jase commented on what a big deal my dad was going to be soon. I agreed but wasn't sure that I cared. As much as that place was my home I knew deep down I was going to leave it someday. I questioned the ritual my dad was going to do on his big night but none of us knew for sure which one was going to be performed.

We finished up our sandwiches and were trying to decide if we wanted to hunt more or call it a day.

Suddenly, a huge gator appeared on the right side of Toby! We hadn't heard a thing. Before any of us could react the gator had him by the arm and was already dragging him down the bank toward the water. Jase and I jumped up and paused for a brief second, shocked by what we were seeing. Then Jase moved quickly, he grabbed the knife out of his pocket and lunged toward the gator! He began stabbing it in the head. I ran over to Toby and grabbed his legs. The gator still hadn't released Toby's arm, it instead began to roll violently back and forth and continued the backward descent toward the water. Toby was flopping back and forth with every forceful thrust the gator made. I still had a hold of his legs but I was struggling to hang on. Suddenly, the gator stopped moving. Jase was laying on his stomach still holding the knife that was pierced into the top of the gators head. Blood was dripping down his hands. I slowly loosened my grip on Toby's legs and moved toward the gators mouth to release Toby's arm. I looked at Jase and he moved his hands down so they would be out of my way. Toby was laying on his back, eyes closed, but he was breathing. I reached my hands into the gators mouth and opened it enough for Jase to pull Toby's pulverized arm out. Toby's arm flopped on the ground and looked like this limp, shredded, large piece of meat. Jase took his shirt off and began to try and wrap it so his arm would hold together in one piece, it looked as though it was hanging on by a few shredded pieces of skin just above the elbow.

We propped him up and let him drape his arms, one good and what was left of the other, over our shoulders so we could get him back and get some help.

By the time we got back to my house Toby had lost a lot of blood. The shirt that Jase had wrapped his arm in was drenched in it. My dad was out on the front porch of the house working on something. I began to holler, he looked up and ran toward us. The look on face said a lot. It wasn't good and we knew it. He had us put him in our truck. Jase and I jumped in the back and my dad drove faster than I ever recall going through the windy trail like road we used to get to the city. Toby was in and out of consciousness the entire ride. When the truck turned onto the paved road I remember the tires squealing as we left the dirt road and went right. It was a ways still to the hospital. I could see through the back window my dad was trying to talk to Toby. Toby's head was laying against the back of the seat and rocking back and forth with the rhythm of the truck, he didn't look good.

Pulling in the entrance to the emergency room caught people's attention. The truck was squealing the entire time we followed the drive to the entrance door. A nurse that was on her way in changed direction and came running over to us. My dad had the door open and Toby in his arms before the nurse reached us. She stayed running ahead of them to open the door.

Jase and I waited in the truck to hear from my dad on how Toby was doing. After what seemed like hours, my dad appeared at the entrance door and waved for us to come in. We were told that Toby had lost too much blood. The Dr. explained he had bled out on the way to the hospital and there was nothing they could do to save him.

We were allowed to bring Toby home.

The ritual was held at the big hall. It was performed by Papa Joseph and every family from the community was there. Toby's mother and father had bathed him that morning. They asked me and Jase to take the wash basin they had used and empty it. I broke down when I saw the color of the water. I can see it as though it was yesterday. It is still so vivid in my mind.

Something changed in me on that day. I felt disconnected from my old self. I wanted to leave the swamps now instead of when I turned eighteen. I was ready for something different. Even though I knew that wasn't going to happen, I started to make some decisions in my head and started planning for my future internally.

The next couple of weeks went by fast. I didn't carry on and do the things I usually did this time of year, everything was different. It was a week away before my dad's big celebration.

Some of the small rituals that lead up to the big event had started. Everyone in the community was involved in some way preparing for it. I took a walk to the big hall one afternoon. On the way I noticed people were sitting outside their homes preparing food or making things like headpieces, necklaces and clothing for the celebration. I sat down next to one of the elders, picked up a piece of wood and began to whittle. He asked me to make a crescent moon. As I whittled sitting under the hot sun I asked questions. I started asking about the celebration. What it meant for my dad. Was it going to change anything for him and I. The man stopped whittling the piece of wood he had been working on, sat up straighter in his chair and looked directly at me. I can still hear his old raspy voice clearly in my head say, Well goodness yes they are going to change son.

On the morning of the big event I woke to squealing outside my bedroom window. I quickly realized it was just the pigs being brought to the big hall for later. Our house was on the dirt path going to the hall so it was getting loud and busy outside. I remember feeling nervous but I wasn't quite sure why. When I got out of bed I could see my dad out on the deck outside my window on his knees with his face planted in the palm of his hands. I figured he was preparing. I got up and went to get something to eat and noticed lots of people outside going to and coming from the hall bringing things.

As the day wore on, the excitement grew. People were sticking their heads in the windows of our house as they passed by. Some had their faces painted and different ritual clothing on. If you weren't from there it would have probably been quite a frightening site.

A few more hours went by and day was turning to night. I was sitting on the front deck looking out over the swamp. Mist was coming off the swamp in a graceful manner. I could hear the music in the distance, our people called it music of the black Indians, and the smell of smoke was in the air. One of the elder men stopped as he was passing to tell me it was time, so I followed behind him down the path. As we got closer to the hall I could see the flames from torches and see shadows of all the people. We walked past two of the pigs hanging in a tree near the entrance to the outside open area of the hall. I was immediately approached by a woman who handed me a drink. I didn't know what it was but after the first sip knew that it was something I had never had before. The atmosphere was frantic. People were drinking and laughing. There were more torches than I had ever seen and small fires lain out that people were jumping over and dancing around in a crazy fashion. The chickens even seemed to be acting out of sort, running around and pecking at each other. Almost as if every living thing knew something big was about to happen.

Papa Joseph appeared on top of the big stump near the water's edge. He stood quietly for some time and then blew something into the fire in front of him that made it crackle loudly and the flames shoot up toward the sky. That got everyone's attention. All of the people stopped what they were doing, stopped the music, grew quiet and turned their attention to Papa Joseph. He took a deep breath and straightened his stance. He began his speech with a welcome to all and went into what a special night this was. He started describing my father and his importance to this night and this ritual. After some more talking, a large human size thing dressed in a black winged suit came walking from behind Papa Joseph. It looked like a huge bird. Everyone got down on one knee and those of us that didn't know we were supposed to, followed the others lead and did the same. Papa Joseph did not turn and look at the winged thing approaching from behind, he continued speaking with a raised voice. He then took the machete from his waste and raised it above his head. Everyone went from kneeling to sitting. The winds seemed to pick up and the bottle tree behind me started clanging. I looked around and caught Jase's stare looking at me. He looked terrified. I didn't understand his look. We had been to many different rituals with similar things happening but his gaze toward me was freaking me out to be honest. The large bird started running around in a senseless fashion.

People dressed in costume and painted up faces and bodies who were standing by Papa Joseph joined in the idiotic dance. Papa continued his stance with the machete held high above his head. The music began to play, people were pouring more drinks. I hadn't taken but a couple drinks of mine and someone came by and filled it back to the rim. The woman next to me took the bottom of my cup and shoved it to my mouth ordering me to drink. I did and then she filled it up again and repeated the command for me to drink. Before I was half way through my second cup I began to feel funny. Everything looked distorted, things were moving in slow motion and my entire body was tingling. I didn't know what was happening but I knew it had something to do with what I was drinking. I let the cup fall out of my hand, I watched it fall and hit the ground. The red liquid sprayed on my shoes and the bottom of my pant legs. My legs felt shaky and I tried to stand. The woman who had insisted I drink grabbed my arm and pulled me up, then the man with her picked me up and threw me over his shoulders. My head bounced off of his back as he walked. I remember others starting to notice as he walked me toward where Papa Joseph was. Everything was so blurry I was having a hard time making out what things were. The man laid me down on the ground in front of Papa Joseph.

Looking up at him was making me dizzy, he looked as though there were two of him and the two of him were moving in a trippy way. The big black feathered thing started jumping over me, back and forth, over and over again. My stomach was barely hanging on, I was sure I was going to be sick. Finally the human looking bird stopped and stood right over top of me. It was looking straight up toward the sky. Then, I was being splashed with something wet. It sprayed on my face and hands. I looked up at Papa Joseph at the same moment he was bringing the machete down on top of the black costumed things head. Blood was squirting all over. I realized that is what was spraying all over me! I raised my hands and put them in front of my face. I tried to sit up but Papa Joseph put his foot on my chest preventing me. I looked to my side and Jase was almost right up to my face, he was crying and telling me how sorry he was and that he was not allowed to tell me anything. I tried pushing my boots into the dirt and scooting forward but at that moment the black winged thing fell directly on top of me. I began to yell. Two men came and picked the thing up by its arms and let more blood spill onto me. Then two other men in costume came behind me and grabbed me under the arms and started dragging me to a chair that had been placed by the water's edge. They sat me down on it but kept hold of my arms, one on each side. I was struggling to hold my head up.

Papa Joseph begin speaking in a gibberish I didn't understand. Then it turned back into our normal language. He was saying he now has a very strong spirit guide. That his father's sacrifice will help us in ways we don't even know yet, and his son will reap the knowledge he possessed before death. I remember that moment...the moment I realized that it was my father that was dressed in the bird costume. Realizing immediately as well that he was dead. That he had just been killed right in front of me. I was so spacey I knew these things but had no emotion about it. I didn't know what was coming next.

What happened next was Papa Joseph finishing the ritual with reciting chants while standing over me. He at times would have his hand on top of my head and other times making symbols in the blood I was drenched in. The people watching were crazed with excitement. The atmosphere was chaotic and scary.

The night eventually ended. I woke the next morning feeling quite ill. My head pounded and my stomach was queasy. I was in my home and was told I could remain there and that my new teachings were going to start soon. Not that day or the one after but soon I was told.

Not long after that night, maybe a few weeks later, I ran. I ran out of the swamps with the clothes on my back, a jug of water and some food in a backpack. I spent a night in the swamps before going into the city.

I wandered around for probably a week before getting picked up by the police. I didn't share what had happened just that my dad had died and I was forced to leave and didn't have anywhere to go. I ended up in foster care until I was eighteen. I worked for a while and then figured continuing my education was the best thing I could do for myself. I learned a lot about the world in the four years I spent with different foster families. Learned how to behave civilized mostly. Anytime I retreated back to ways I knew, I would know it immediately just by the look on people's faces and I would correct it right away. I went off to college and started my life anew. And not too long after that I met you guys. You all have changed my life for the better in so many ways and I thank you for that.

We were all silent for a moment. Then one at a time moved over to Jackson and hugged him. None of us spoke, we just sat for a moment and held each other.

The Climb

I set one of my feet on the first step, then allow my other foot to join and look up at the stairs ascending into the sky. The stairs go on as far as the eye can see. Kora appears on my right side. We give each other a look of reassurance and take our next step together. I turn to look behind me to make sure the others are there, but they are not. There is nothing behind me, not even the ground! There is nothing but clouds all around me and the stairs in front of me. I yell for Kora who is no longer next to me either. The air is quiet. No wind or noise can be heard. I take another step and it is the same view. I feel panicked and begin climbing as fast as I can, yelling for the others as I do. After a minute of this I stop, still nothing. Until, without warning, a strong wind comes roaring from behind.

The sound is like a train hammering down the tracks at eighty miles an hour. It is blowing so strong I am scared it is going to blow me right off the stairs. I grab hold of the rail and wrap my arms tightly around until it stops.

When the wind stops, I hear Kora. She is yelling for me. I yell back over and over, I can't tell where her voice is coming from. It echoes all around me. As I begin to stand back up I hear Isaac. He is yelling for me to climb faster. He sounds frantic. I start climbing again as fast as I can. I continue looking behind me, each time into nothingness. Then I notice a smell. It is so pungent it makes my stomach turn and feel nauseous. I look behind me once again and trip as I take my next step. My head bounces on the stair in front of me and I land on my side grabbing hold of the rail to stop myself from falling. I hear Isaac's voice yelling again. Then, something grabs my leg. I flip over on my back and look down. It is Kora! My heart is in my throat. I stretch my arm out for her to grab. As she reaches her arm up for me I can see something has a hold of her around her waist! It is a long, thin arm. The fingers are dirty and the nails are jabbing into Kora's stomach. I stretch myself further and try to grab hold of the arm to get it off of her. Kora is screaming and struggling to keep her position on the stair she is on. Whatever has a hold of her is trying to pull her back. We both are struggling to get her free. The hand moves from gripping her stomach to the back of her head and grabs hold of her hair.

Kora screams even louder as this hand pulls back on her hair until her body is arched. I move down a step and kick as hard as I can right above the hand hoping I will hit whatever it is. My foot makes contact with something, there is this awful squealing noise that follows. It releases its grip on Kora. We quickly move up the stairs, looking behind us as we go.

The two of us climb for a bit. Whatever that thing was has not come back...yet anyway. We test the steps to see if we can go back down. We can move down one step but then feel nothing for our foot to set on beyond that. We still cannot see anything, there is a heavy fog that blocks our view. The stairs are still visible in front of us, still seeming endless.

Kora and I stand still in one spot for a few moments. Then, Kora points out something in flight quite a ways in front of us. It looks beautiful. It is a goldish color and sparkles in the sky as it turns direction in flight. "Wow." Kora says.

"What is that?" I wondered out loud.

We watch as it gets closer. "It looks like an angel." Kora whispers.

It swoops down even closer. It is the most brilliant gold color and has the shape of a person. It looks like wings extending out on the side but we can't get a good look at what it is. It is mostly color. The brightest, most radiant color I have ever seen.

This thing begins to move gently until it is directly in front of us. We stand frozen looking at it. I have the most peaceful feeling. It continues to float in one spot. I feel as though I am in a trance. I cannot turn my head to look away nor do I want to. Suddenly, it darts upward and disappears. We continue staring in the direction it left. Immediately, the feeling in the air changes. It goes right back to an uneasy, chilling feeling.

As we begin climbing again and look up, we see Isaac who is just a few steps ahead of us. He is staring off to his right at something. We move up to where he is and nudge him. He turns and looks at us, he has the biggest smile on his face. "Look." He says and points off in the direction he is focused on. Off in the distance it looks like Jackson and Sophie. I squint my eyes to try and see them better.

"What are they doing?" I ask. "How are they not on the stairs?"

Isaac answers without turning his head to look at me. "They are flying."

It does look like they are flying I thought. They are getting further and further away from us.

"Amazing!" Kora exclaimed.

All of a sudden, there is a squealing noise. It sounds like it is coming from behind us. We turn in unison to look. It is foggy but I can see something coming up the stairs.

I realize as it gets close that it is one of the nuns from St. Jude's institute! We all jump up a step at the same exact time. Kora grabs hold of my arm. A distorted looking Sister Margie is clambering up the stairs on all fours, her legs and arms imitating the crawl of a spider. Her long black dress is flapping in the wind around her. She begins moving so fast we don't have time to react other than stay frozen in fear where we stand. Isaac moves down a step acting as though he is going to protect us, just like he used to at the asylum. When she reaches us, she contorts her body to move on the outside of the stairs avoiding us entirely. As she passes, she looks us over from top to bottom. I can't breathe and my heart feels like it has stopped. Her face is contorted and grayish in color. Her eyes look sunken into her head. As she studies each of us her head moves up and down in a creepy, slow motion fashion. Once she passes, she instantly disappears. It takes a few moments after she is out of site for my shoulders that are lifted stiff up to my ears to slowly drop back down.

We stand still and focus on slowing our breathing. I turn to look at Isaac who is again focused on something. He is staring up ahead with a curious look on his face. I turn back forward to see what he is looking at. There are balloons floating, hundreds of balloons, in all different colors. I can see that Kora has noticed them as well now. Kora looks confused. "I know this." She says.

"What?" Isaac asks.

"It looks like my birthday party when I was ten. My mom had gotten hundreds of balloons that were filled with helium. Every balloon had a string tied to the bottom of them. I had lots of kids over to my house for the party. The entire living room of our house was filled with these balloons. All of us kids got to grab as many as we could and brought them to the back yard. My mom had us stand in a circle and make a wish in our heads and said the balloons would carry the wishes all the way up to heaven. We could wish for anything, even what my mom would call Santa Claus wishes. If our wishes didn't come true then they just weren't meant to be. So we should not be upset my mom told us. We counted down from ten and then all of us at the same time let go of our balloons. It looked just like this. Just like this."

Isaac and I turned our focus back to the balloons floating. They looked so cool. Eventually, they all disappear just like Sister Margie did. Isaac pushes his way between Kora and I and starts up the stairs again. I follow, and Kora follows behind me. After just a few more steps something else appears. It looks like paint. Different colors rolling in the sky as though the paint is dancing. It is forming different symbols as it floats. Isaac leans up against the railing looking intently. "We used those symbol in our services." He says almost to himself. "We would paint them on our bodies. They have different meanings. It depended on what the service was for as to what symbol we would use. I wonder if Jackson had used any of these in his cult like living."

"What is that hook looking one used for?" Kora asked him.

"It was used as protection against demons."

"Is this supposed to be our lives flashing before our eyes?" I ask.

Isaac looks at me and smiles, not his usual ear to ear grin but a small up-turned mouth smile. "This is supposed to be the biggest event of our short lives. I guess we need to embrace it and survive it and learn from it. There must be a point to all of it. Let's pay attention to everything we see and hear. Maybe we can sort it out on the other side." He ends with his usual ear to ear grin, which was actually comforting.

The wind starts to swirl and the sky initiates another surprise for us. Snow, wet looking leaves, rain and pollen begin to fall. It looks stunning. I turn in a circle on the step I am on and look all around fascinated with what is happening. I wonder what it means. Is this the big reveal of the season we have chosen?... I wondered. But this is all the seasons falling gracefully from above. There is probably all kinds of things that are going to be different from what we think we know.

Then suddenly it is just leaves. Leaves and the smell of a freshly lit fire. "Oh God." I say.

Isaac and Kora look at me but don't speak. But it isn't the memory I thought it was going to be. Without warning, this white fur ball is running down the stairs at us. "Roxy?" I say.

"Your dog?" Isaac asks.

"From when I was like twelve!" I exclaim. "Roxy was a medium size, white mutt. She came from the pound as a puppy when I was probably two years old and she was hit and killed by a car when I was around twelve. I was heart broke. We buried her in the backyard and I remember I kept putting leaves on top of the freshly dug up ground. I was scared somebody was going to dig her up and take her. I don't have a clue why I thought that."

"Awww." Kora says. "She is so cute."

Roxy is bouncing around on the stairs. Tail wagging and tongue hanging out. I reach out to touch her head and she pounces up the stairs and fades away.

After more climbing, the fog thickens even more so. The air turns cold and the wind becomes silent. A small tapping noise is coming from somewhere ahead of us. It sounds like something is tapping on a stair. We don't move. The noise starts getting louder until it seems to be just a step above us. The fog allows us to peer through and see what it is. A man with a knife appears in front of us. He is tapping the weapon on the rail in a rhythmic motion. Kora grabs my arm. "Is that your father?" I ask her under my breath.

"I never knew my father, but he looks a lot like the man that killed my mother." She answered louder than I expected.

I looked at Kora and she has her eyes are locked on him. "Move asshole!" Isaac yells.

"Isaac!" I say and grab his arm.

Isaac shrugs me off. "I don't give a shit. These asshole images from the past are starting to be in the way of what we are trying do here. We have a destination to get to." He takes a step toward the man who has not moved. As he reaches him the man raises the knife above his head. Isaac stops suddenly. I watch as the knife swipes down toward Isaac's chest. Right before it makes impact it dissipates. I inhale deeply and grab Koras hand. Isaac lowers his head and I can tell takes a deep breath of his own.

After climbing a while longer we sit and rest. We all wonder how and where Sophie and Jackson are and if they are ok. We had decided to all climb up the same slide but we had not seen them since the start. While we are looking around at our surroundings more things appear and disappear. We watch the things that are coming and going with complete vigilance. Every image and memory that comes, we enjoy and talk about. Even the scary ones, we now realize can't hurt us, so we watch. It seems like a revisiting of our lives. Important, horrifying and special times seen again but not able to touch us in the way they once did.

Kora's mother, the last thing we see, evaporates into the clouds. The sky clears, the sun shines down on us and we see what looks like the top of the slide. "Let's do this." Kora says. Isaac and I follow her up the last set of steps.

At the Bottom

It is eerily quiet. The air is quite brisk, and it smells of fall... wet leaves and grass. I pick myself up off of the cool ground, look down at my friends and then around at my surroundings. We are in a wooded area. Everyone else is still lying on the ground, including Jackson and Sophie. I walk around to each of them and shake them lightly, one at a time until everyone is up. Their reaction looks exactly like mine, everyone is scanning the location we have landed in.

We sit in silence. Nobody talks or moves. If someone would have told me that this would become a reality for me I would have never believed them. There are things you acknowledge. Things you hear of, speak of, fear and have a curiosity for. But to actually be in the state of things and to find that they actually exist as opposed to an idea of them is difficult to take in to say the least.

"It appears we have landed in fall." Isaac says as he begins to stand and stretch.

"Yeah. Feels like it too." I say. "At least we thought to layer our sweatshirts and longer pants over top of our summer wear." Ending my statement with the best fake smile I can muster.

"Alright, Where to?" Kora wants to know right away.

None of us know how to answer that. How could we, we don't even know where we are. Or better yet, we don't know whose season it is that we are in. Maybe it is more than one of ours, it really is impossible to say. The answer to Kora's question comes from Jackson who explains that we should just pick a direction to walk and start walking. And so that is what we do. There are trails going in all directions, we head out on one of them.

There are leaves scattered all over the ground and still lots on the trees. Dull red, orange and yellows. Not vibrant or beautiful at all. There is a strange variety of trees growing next to each other.

Hardwood, softwood, redwood, palm trees and all sorts of other trees that don't belong together. Some of the leaves are crunching under our feet and some are soft and sticking to our shoes. We continue walking on the same trail for a couple of hours I would guess but time feels different here.

Even though none of us have eaten since morning, nobody feels hungry. We haven't given any thought about what we could eat so we aren't paying any attention to what possibilities may be along the trail or in the woods.

We come across a creek, sitting back not far from the path we are on. Isaac thinks we should stay along-side it, so we do. It takes us off our path but we continue following anyway. The water is cold and running swiftly. There are large boulders sticking up in the shallows of the water. It reminds me of a spot we used to swim at back home, where the river runs into Lake Superior.

As the five of us continue walking, following the creek we hear a noise. It is faint but we all hear it. "That sounds like someone struggling to breath." Jackson says.

"What is that?" Sophie asks almost simultaneously.

"Listen." Jackson says in a low whisper.

We stop walking and stand still. Then hear it again and it definitely is the sound of a person wheezing.

I begin looking in all directions to see where the noise came from. I don't see anything. I can feel panic setting in and my heart begins to pound. I try breathing slow, deep breaths and remind myself that we chose to do this, knowing full well this might not be an easy thing.

The five of us have unintentionally formed this shoulder to shoulder circle facing outward, all of us scanning the woods around us. Then, I see movement out of the corner of my right eye, it comes from behind a tree that is almost right in front of me. "There!" I say louder than I had intended, and point in the direction of the tree. Everyone turns in their spot and focuses on the tree. It looks like a thin, wrinkled hand resting on the side of the very old looking tree, about five feet up. We can't see anything but the hand, whatever is attached lies behind the large trunk, hidden from our view. None of us move an inch, or take a breath for that matter. My eyes are completely focused on this thin, wrinkled hand, along with everyone else's. After a few seconds or so the hand moves into a fist and then back to its original position. Now, the fingers begin to crawl up the tree, in a slow motion movement. One wrinkled finger after another crawling with a purpose. The other hand appears on the opposite side of the trunk, it comes around the tree trunk and more of the arm becomes visible, it matches the hand in its thin, wrinkled appearance. I imagine how long the arms must be in order to wrap around the trunk. Now, long, ashy colored, stringy hair drapes onto the part of the arm that we can see.

Suddenly, this thing starts climbing the tree so fast and furious around the trunk over and over until it is at the top and out of sight! The entire body was so thin and the arms and legs looked abnormally long. The grotesque thing was wearing some sort of torn up cloth dress that looked dated to the 1600's. I look around at the others and they are all staring with their heads tilted up, looking at the top of the tree. After a minute of all of us continuing to stare at the top of the tree, I ask, "Can we go now?"

"Yes please." Kora responds.

"We need to stick together. I do not believe splitting up like we had considered before we got here would be wise." Jackson states.

"No way!" Sophie said. "I have a feeling that thing isn't going to be the only weird thing we witness here. I'm not so sure this was a good idea after all."

"Kind of late for that now!" Isaac yells loudly.

Jackson takes a couple of steps forward, toward the tree that thing had just climbed. "Let's keep moving." He says. "We need to pay attention for anything that would help us know who we are here to help."

All of us began walking again, away from the tree, and back in the direction we were going before we stopped.

We continue walking in the same direction the creek is flowing. It is difficult to get a sense of time, I am not sure how long we have been hiking and I don't think I am alone with this feeling. Sophie mentioned the same thing a little while ago.

Isaac suddenly slows his pace and points out that it looks like the water in the creek is starting to flow faster. We turn and look behind us. The creek itself seems to be widening before our eyes. "What the hell?" Jackson says. Suddenly, I feel my feet getting wet. I look down and see water pouring over the tops of my shoes.

"What is happening?" I whisper out loud. Then I hear a strange noise, it sounds like a bathtub filling up with water, but much louder.

"Grab on to each other!" Isaac yells.

Quickly, we do as Isaac says. I turn to look back and see a raging river heading right at us! The water hits us so hard and fast I can't keep hold of Sophie's arm. My hand is immediately ripped off of her and I am swept along in the water. I have no control but keep trying to get my body facing forward with my feet in front of me. It is so difficult, the water is running so fast. As I churn in the water, mostly out of control, my head continues to submerge over and over again. I am struggling to keep myself from ramming into the massive boulders that are basically everywhere. I notice a tree laying in the water up ahead. I kick my legs and paddle my arms with as much strength as I can muster to position myself to be in the direct path that the tree is.

I get over far enough and now I'm heading straight for it. I put my arms out in front of me to try and soften the impact. It doesn't help, I hit hard. My arms are thrown over the top of the log and my chest takes the brunt of the hit. My right leg gets hooked in between one of the branches that is laying underneath the water. The branch seems to grab hold and now I am stuck! The force of the water is continuing to try and push me down stream while my leg is being held so I struggle as I am trying not to allow myself to be submerged under.

Then, I get hit hard from behind and it dislodges my foot. It's Isaac. He grabs hold of me and we continue flowing downstream. We are spinning in circles, turning in all directions. As I look ahead I can see that the water is going to turn calm almost instantly, there is not so much as a ripple in the water. Thank God, I think, I don't know how much longer I can keep my head above water. Within seconds, we flow into the still water.

I hear someone yell... it's Sophie! She is standing on the shore waving at us. Isaac and I struggle to swim over, we are absolutely exhausted. Finally, we reach the edge of the river, my body gives out now that it can. I plop my arms on the sand, my legs are still submerged in the water but I need to catch my breath before moving another inch. Isaac is next to me doing the same. Sophie walks over and sits down by us. She is soaked and looks as fatigued as us.

She looks our way and says. "I can't get a grasp on this place. Is this trickery, magic or something evil?"

"Maybe it's all of the above." Isaac answered.

"Did either one of you see Jackson or Kora?" I ask.

Sophie started to sob. "Jackson had my hand for a long time. The water was throwing us around like rag dolls. We ran into a boulder and Jackson's hand was gone from mine in an instant. I tried to see where he was but never even got a glimpse. The water was rising and falling in swells blocking my view of anything, he could have been two feet from me. I lost Kora's arm right away, as soon as the first gush of water hit. She was ahead of us when I saw her last." Her eyes drift forward. "JACKSON!" She screams.

Sure enough, Jackson is on the other side of the river. He is walking toward the river's edge when he must hear Sophie's screams, he stops walking and looks in our direction. I watch as he falls to his knees and put his hands to his face. Sophie jumps up and leaps back in the water. "Sophie stop!" Jackson hollers. "I will come to that side!" She stops swimming and floats where she is until Jackson reaches her and they swim back together. The two lay down as soon as they reach dry land, facing each other with looks of disbelief and relief on their faces.

I start scanning the beach and notice something down from where we are.

"Now what is that?" I say out loud as I begin to walk and then run toward what looks like a body not too far down from us. It is a body... Kora! She is lying face down in the sand. I fall to my knees on the ground next to her and check to see if she is breathing. "She is breathing!" I turn and tell the others who have caught up and are now standing behind me.

"Thank the Lord." Jackson says

"Thank whoever the hell is listening!" Isaac says.

We all sit down next to Kora to make sure she is going to be alright. She begins to cough and spit up water. I set my hand on her back. "We are all here Kora. Try to relax and catch your breath." I feel as though I mumbled the words but Kora nods her head, so I assume she grasps what I said.

We don't move until everyone feels like they have their senses back. It is starting to get dark. We barely discuss the couple of bizarre incidents, they were almost expected I thought. It is well known that this place is not like our own, where we came from. So far, it is living up to its reputation.

The five of us decide we will spend the night on the river bank. It has gotten too dark for us to continue roaming. I thought for a moment about us staying so close to the water, that it may not be such a great idea, in case the river was to rise and flood again.

But, with everything we have experienced here so far, we probably wouldn't be completely safe anywhere. Jackson is able to build a fire and we all lay around it, warming up and drying our clothes.

I did not remember falling asleep or waking at all during the night. I feel quite rested. Everyone else is already up. They have all moved away from the river a bit, I'm assuming so they wouldn't wake me. I get up, walk over to join them and say my good mornings. Once I sit down I notice something odd. The scar that Isaac had down the left side of his face is no longer there. I mention it to Isaac. He of course hasn't noticed... he has not been in front of a mirror since we arrived. He brought his hand up and felt the side of his face where it was indented from a lashing he had as a child. The look on his face said it all. "How is my scar gone?" Isaac looks around at all of us as he asks.

"I haven't been able to understand or explain anything since we got here," Jackson answers, "I don't think I want to start with trying to explain that."

"Maybe there is some kind of healing power here." Sophie offers. "After all, it is quite magical."

The rest of us check any scar or flaw we had attained in our lifetime. Gone. They are all gone...on all of us...gone. As we stand checking ourselves and each other Isaac notices and points out a man walking toward us.

When the man is close, he looks us over and says, "Some people believe it is the water. That it heals us. One of the first things that happens when you get here is the river floods. Some believe it cleanses and heals us. Like a baptism in a way"

"Who are you?" I ask the man

"My name is Joshua."

"What are you doing here?"

"I live here. This is my home. And I hope you all will have a pleasant stay."

"We aren't staying!" Isaac blurted out. "Just visiting for a time, a short time." The man laughed and continued laughing as he walked away.

"Should we stop him?" Kora asks

"What for?" Isaac says with a bit of sarcasm.

"Um, maybe to ask questions we would like answers to about this place."

"Everyone here needs to figure out what their purpose is by themselves." Isaac answers.

Kora looks irritated with him but exhales deeply and turns away.

This place is so strange. I had tried to mentally prepare myself while making the decision to climb the slide but I don't think one could have really prepared themselves for what is happening. The five of us decide to move from this spot by the river. We have no idea where we are going or who we are looking for so hopefully whatever or whoever it is will come up and hit us in the face.

We begin to walk again, away from the river this time, into the forest. The forest is so thick with trees it prevents most sunshine from getting through, which makes it quite dark and drab. After following the trail for a short time it suddenly disappears. What was a trail is hidden under fallen tree limbs, branches and leaves...lots of leaves. It makes it really hard to see and follow.

As we move forward there is lots of crunching noise all around us. I'm sure there are all kinds of animals in these woods but it gives us an uneasy feeling, not knowing what is making the sounds. We continue deeper in and Sophie notices a beautiful pure white deer standing straight ahead in our direct path. We all stop and take notice. It is exquisite. The perfectly symmetrical horns coming from the top of the animals head are the same color white as the rest of it. "Look." I say and point at the black raven perched on the tree next to this stunning creature. It appears to be watching us.

The raven is black as night and just as perfect as the deer in its healthy looking state. It is perched on the end of a branch when it begins to flap its wings and leave the tree. It flies in a circle then positions itself without deviation right in front of the white deer's nose. The deer lifts its head as if to acknowledge what the raven has to say. The raven stays hovering this way for what seems like a long time before flying off.

The deer turns and looks at us. At first it stares as though it is wondering why we were intruding on its conversation but then nods its head up and down, turns and begins walking away from where we stand.

"Let's follow it." Jackson says.

"Why?" Kora asks

"I think it wants us to. I think it is here to help in some way."

Isaac takes a few steps ahead following the deer and looks back our way. "I think Jackson is right." He says.

As we continue following behind the white deer, the fog in the forest thickens until, it is hard to see the deer that isn't more than ten feet ahead of us.

Then suddenly we notice a huge black cloud forming in the sky above us.

We realize immediately that it is not a cloud. And within seconds we know what it is, a swarm of ravens. They begin diving at us! It is so frightening. We try to run but it is no use, we cannot get away. I notice the white deer disappear in the fog.

"Stay together!" Jackson yells.

I begin to run back toward Jackson when I am lifted off the ground. I have no idea how many ravens have a hold of me but I continue getting higher and higher soaring above the treetops. I hear the others yelling and screaming. When I look down, I no longer see anything, not the ground or the tops of the trees. There is nothing but a fog until…everything goes black.

Spring

I open my eyes. My mind is in a fog and I'm confused for a moment. Then I realize I am laying in a field of wildflowers. The smell is sweet and citrusy. I see the others near me. They are sitting up and looking around as well.

"This works." Sophie says in a low voice.

"No doubt." I agree.

A group of butterflies pass by my head. I can hear birds singing, the wind is warm and blowing softly. This place looks so lovely.

"Wow." Kora exclaims.

Just then, a group of wild horses appear over the top of a hill that is off in the distance. They begin heading our way. I watch as their manes flow in a slow motion movement behind their heads as they gallop across the field.

"What beautiful creatures." I say.

The closer they get, the louder the rumbling sound. The entire ground beneath me feels like it is vibrating. One of the horses gets so close to me, I feel like I could reach out and touch it. As they pass by, I notice one of them has rope hanging from around its neck. I wondered if it had a rider that may have fallen off. Or maybe someone was trying to catch it.

"Amazing new place. As cool as this all is guys…where are we?" Jackson asks.

"Not quite sure." Isaac answers. "But, I would guess we are definitely in spring."

Kora jumps up from where she is sitting. "Ya think." She says and laughs. "I'm just glad that wasn't a group of scary nuns charging toward us!"

All of us chuckle.

"Or ravens." Isaac mumbles.

Our mood obviously or strangely adjusts to our surroundings. As soon as we see that things look pleasant we are at ease. When that changes so does our frame of mind. I think how odd that is and how uncontrolled I feel it is.

It's almost instant and without consideration. If any of the things we had encountered so far had happened before climbing the slides it would have taken time to move past the awful experience. The reality of the situation would be felt for a time far beyond the actual event. Then I wondered, maybe this isn't real. Maybe this is a dream. But I knew that wasn't the case. It felt very real. I feel like I need to just deal with the situation I put myself in and hope it will all make sense when we have accomplished what we think we have to do here.

We get up and discuss which way to go. We decide to head in the direction the horses had come from. As we walk in that direction and get close to the hill the horses came over we see a huge apple orchard on the other side. There are apple trees as far as the eye can see.

"I have never seen so many apple trees." I mention.

Sophie starts to run ahead. Kora follows her. They are skipping and laughing. Maybe this place will be a healing thing for us, I thought. Sophie yells something and points. I try to see what it is.

"Bicycles!" Kora yells.

Sophie and her take off running toward them.

"What the heck?" Jackson mutters.

When Jackson, Isaac and I get to the bikes Sophie and Kora are already riding on one, a tandem bike. There are three more. Another tandem and two one seaters. They are each a different color, all pastels. They all have nice fat, comfortable looking seats. Kora is in the front of the one her and Sophie are on.

They are both peddling and pretty much going in circles around one of the apple trees laughing and squealing.

I hurry and grab the pretty pastel pink tandem and won't let anyone else on with me. Isaac and Jackson grab the other two and we begin to ride through the orchard cutting each other off and racing across the field. The sun feels wonderful shining down on my face. The field is full of hills which makes it so much fun on these bikes.

As I pedal along, leading the pack of bikers, I notice we have left the orchard. There are no more apple trees. No more flowers either. I slow my peddling and stop all together. The others come up alongside me. The field has turned into mostly long grass. We do notice a structure of some sort quite a ways ahead. I get off the bike and stretch my arms and legs. "Should we continue going this way?" I ask.

"It's as good a way as any." Jackson says. "Since we have no clue where we are or where we should be going." He ends his statement with a crooked smile.

"Quite true." I acknowledge.

Jackson races over to my pretty, pastel pink bike and takes off on it. I holler but he won't stop. "He took my bike." I tell the others with a playful frown on my face. We all jump on the remaining bikes and try to catch up with him. This time I am riding in the back with Sophie steering in the front on the pastel green tandem. On the end of the handle bars on each bike is a mirror.

I look in the mirror on the right handle bar and watch as Isaac gains on us.

"He is catching us!" I tell Sophie.

"Peddle faster." She yells back.

We laugh as we peddle as fast as our legs will allow. Then I move my eyes back to the mirror to make sure we have put some distance between ourselves and Isaac. As I look into the mirror, the reflection of what I see makes me quickly pull my eyes away. It wasn't Isaac. I can't help it and look back into the mirror. It's a young teenage girl. She looks dead. She is grayish in color and her hair and clothes are wet. There are tiny flowers stuck in parts of her matted hair. Her eyes stare back into mine and look despondent. I look away and holler at Sophie to stop.

"What's wrong?" Sophie asks as she turns her head back to try and see me.

I look to the mirror again and it is Isaac with his huge smile. I lay my head on Sophie's back.

"I saw something in the mirror. It wasn't Isaac. I don't know who or what it was."

"Let's stop for a minute." She offers and starts slowing down.

I lift my head and begin to tell her but as my eyes go to the mirror, it is the dead looking girl almost directly behind our back tire! I scream and twist my body to look behind me. It makes the bike go out of control and we wipe out. The bike lands on my legs.

I hurry and throw it off and scoot away looking all around, trying to see where the girl went. But, there is no girl. Isaac had to hurry and steer around us so he didn't hit us from behind. Everyone else gets to where we fell and stops.

"Are you ok?" Kora asks. "What happened?"

"What did you see?" Sophie asks.

"I don't know." I am still sitting on the ground looking all around. "When I looked in the mirror, there was a girl. It wasn't Isaac. She looked dead! She was all wet and bloated."

"What." Isaac says loudly. "What do you mean? Where is she? What did she look like?"

I suddenly realize what Isaac is thinking. "Oh Isaac, I don't know if it was your sister. I pulled my eyes away so quickly once I saw her."

"Who else here has someone who has anything in common with what you saw!" Isaac yells. "She must need my help. Why didn't she let ME see her! "How do I help you!" He yells. Isaac starts to turn in a circle while standing in one spot continuously yelling. "AHHHHH!"

Jackson goes up to him and grabs him by the shoulders. "Isaac! Isaac stop for a minute. Stop Isaac! Listen please."

Isaac stops and looks at Jackson. His eyes are already red from crying. The tears are flowing freely down his cheeks. He collapses to his knees and looks straight ahead.

"How are we supposed to help our loved ones if they disappear as fast as they appear? How are we supposed to know what to do?"

Jackson sits down next to him. "We don't know. All we can do is deal with what comes our way the best we can. Maybe that was just a quick intro to your sister letting you know how to help her. But if it was her, now we know she is here, right. Maybe that was your sign to let you know that is who you are here to help. "

We sit quiet for some time. Then Isaac decides it is time to move on. We follow his lead. Nobody gets on a bike, we just start walking. Nobody is talking. The field seems to go on forever until we notice what looks like a circus tent not very far ahead. Nobody says a word, we just continue walking toward the giant tent. The closer we get, the louder the music is. And it is unquestionably circus sounding music. I notice some miniature horses by the side of the tent. There are about six of them and they are grazing on the grass. My eyes scan the area all around the tent as we approach. The only other thing I notice outside is an adorable little puppy. It is hopping around playfully with what looks like a blue beach ball. As we round to the front entrance there is a man standing inside of a ticket booth.

Jackson walks up to him and I can see they are talking.

After a few minutes Jackson rejoins us and tells us we do not get to go in, that they are sold out.

"Interesting." Sophie comments. "Sold out?" Could you see inside?" She asks.

"No. That was the weird thing, the entrance was open but it was just black, I couldn't see anything."

"To hell with it then." I say. "Let's keep moving."

"No!" Sophie yells. "I want to go in."

We all turn and look at Sophie. Jackson moves to her side. "What's going on?"

"It's the one good memory I have of my mother. She took me to a circus when I was about ten. One of the occasions she was allowed to be in the real world for a short time."

Just then a man, woman and three children exit from the tent. The man walks over to Sophie and hands her five tickets. He says, "Here you go honey. You take your friends. We have seen this show many times." Then they walk away and disappear.

I walk up to Sophie and grab her hand and we head toward the open entrance of the tent. It smells of cotton candy and buttered popcorn. As we enter the blackness fades and an arena shows itself in the middle with bleacher seats all around. There are three elephants in the arena standing tall on the dirt floor.

They are standing on their massive back legs and tower over the small man standing in front of them. I look around at the seats and they are empty. The man standing in the arena with the elephants takes a bow as though there is an audience. Great, I think to myself.

I look over to Sophie and she looks terrified. "What is going on?" I ask her.

She is scanning the seats like I was. She looked at me and said. "We shouldn't be here."

"You wanted to come in Sophie! I don't understand. What's going on?" I say.

Before she can answer me a voice comes from the middle of the arena. The man and the three giant elephants are no longer there. There is now a man dressed in a red suit with a red top hat and he is speaking into a microphone. He looks our way and begins to announce the next performers. He starts with…"Ladies and Gentlemen, please give a big round of applause for our next performer…the beautiful, the most talented and most requested fortune teller the world has ever seen…Ms. Voncille Elizabeth!"

"Why does that name sound familiar." I say out loud.

Sophie looks at me and says, "Because it is my mom."

"Aunt Beth?" I say. A light bulb goes off in my head. I never think about her real name, she has always just went by Beth. "Aunt Beth thought she could see the future right? She said she could speak to the dead."

"Yeah." Sophie replies. "Then she ended up in a mental hospital."

"I know." I grab Sophie by the arm. "Come on, this isn't real. Let's just go."

As I turn her around to go back out there is a clown standing right in the way. The clown puts his hands up above his head and speaks loudly. "Why of course this is real my dear. We only deal with real here."

Then he sticks his arm out and says, "Go ahead, touch. Go ahead! See for yourself."

"We don't need to touch you to know." I tell him.

He glares directly at me, "I wasn't talking to you Miss non believer, now was I." He moves his glare to Sophie. "You don't want to talk to dear old mom? Hmmm." He looks toward what looks like Aunt Beth. "The false profit in the flesh?"

"Whoever or whatever that is, it's not my mother!" Sophie hollers back at him. "My mother would not be here. She is in a…home." She finishes with.

"A home indeed." The clown smiles wide. "But you see, she left that home. The day she heard you had left yours. That's right dear, she couldn't bear it. As if her mind didn't torture her enough. You just had to add to that. Well, she couldn't handle it. So…she came here."

Sophie glared back at the man in the clown suit. "My mother was crazy! You have no idea what it was like to live with someone or not live with someone who said they spoke to dead people. Don't you dare judge me! My mother hasn't been a part of helping me make decisions in my life for a very long time!"

Suddenly, a loud cheer comes from all around us. I look at the bleachers and they are filled with people. The crowd is roaring in laughter. I look into the arena and there is a group of little dogs doing tricks. I turn back to Sophie and her mother is standing directly behind her. My eyes get big and Sophie must notice this. She whips around and is face to face with her mom. Her mom tries to put her hand up to Sophie's cheek, but Sophie steps back.

"Sophie." Her mother says. "I am so sorry for everything you went through because of me. I shouldn't have done what I did. I didn't know how not to. I am learning the sins of my ways here. You can't help me with that."

"No worries. I'm here supporting my friends, my real family." Sophie replies.

I put my hand on Sophie's back. "Sophie, maybe you should hear her out."

"Celeste." Beth turned toward me. "You have grown into such a lovely young woman."

I smile politely. "Aunt Beth. We are not exactly sure what we are supposed to be doing here. How did you get here?"

"I don't know." She says. "I don't remember. I was at the hospital and I was looking out the window at a flock of birds flying off of the roof."

Sophie grabs my hand. "Come on." She pulls me past her mother toward the others. We start to walk back toward the entrance that we came in.

"Sophie stop, please." I hear her mother yell from behind.

Sophie doesn't stop. But the clown appears in front of the entrance, and now he is holding what looks like a machete. He has an evil smile on his face. "Did mommy tell you your immediate future Sophie?" He Yells and begins to laugh wickedly. His crooked painted on red lips have streaks of red coming down on each side of his mouth now. I can hear the crowd of people cheering and laughing again. We begin backing up as a group.

"That way." Isaac points to the other side of the tent. There is a piece of the tent that we see light from the outside through.

We take off running straight through the arena section. Jackson trips on one of the little dogs and the entire audience comes to their feet with applause. I grab Jackson's hand and help him up... a machete comes down right where he just got up from. The crowd is in a frenzy with their excitement. They are cheering and whistling. The others are already at the opening in the tent. Jackson grabs my arm and we take off again.

But something grabs my ankle and I fall hard, face down on the dirt. The people in the audience erupt in cheers again. I roll over on my back and scream when I see the clown crawling toward me with the machete in between his teeth in his overpainted mouth. Jackson steps toward him and kicks him in the head. The clown rolls on his side from the force of the kick Jackson delivered. We notice Isaac holding the opening of the tent for us, the others must have already went through. My legs are going as fast as they can trying to keep up with Jackson who has hold of my arm again. We don't stop until we are through the opening in the tent wall.

The sun is so bright, initially it blinds me. I fall on the grass and try to focus my eyes. It feels so hot. It feels like summer...

Summer's Story

I feel warm water washing over my feet. I am laying on a beach with sand as white as snow. I sit myself up and look out at the turquoise waters. It is absolutely beautiful. Kora sits up on her knees behind me and lays her head on my shoulder. "Now what?" She asks in a quiet voice.

"Not sure." I answer. "I guess we find out."

The rest of the group is standing and looking around. I jump to my feet and walk into the water. The water is warm and there is a smell of salt is in the air. This place feels familiar. There are large boulder size rocks scattered along the beach. Jackson climbs onto one of the boulders that is sitting in the shallows of the water and stands on top. Isaac runs into the water and plunges himself into a breaking wave that is heading toward the shore. I sit down in the warm water and lean back on my arms with my face tilted up toward the sun. Kora and Sophie join me.

The sound of children laughing brings me out of my peaceful state. I sit up and see a raft floating straight out in front of us. It has barrels underneath and what looks like bamboo as the deck. There sit five children. They are sitting with their legs folded and appear to be paying attention to something that is in the middle of their circle formation. They all have a look of delight on their faces and every so often they all giggle at whatever is on the raft with them. Jackson yells to them a few times but they don't acknowledge him, never so much as turn their heads from whatever it is they are looking at. After a few minutes they have drifted too far away to attempt any kind of contact.

"What do you guys think?" Jackson asks.

Isaac is exiting the water, "I think we should take a walk that way." And points down the beach.

"Sure." Jackson agrees and looks at the rest of us, we nod in agreement as well.

The warm air blows softly as we walk in the direction Isaac suggested. Then, I think I hear music. It is hard to tell, it is so quiet or far away still.

"Do you hear that?" I say to the group as the music seems to be a little closer.

"Hear what?" Sophie asks.

"The music?" Kora says.

"Yes!" I say. "I thought that's what I was hearing. You hear it too?"

"Maybe it's coming from that ice-cream truck." Isaac says as he points down the beach at an ice cream truck speeding toward us.

"Likely possibility." Jackson says with a look of concern on his face.

As the truck gets closer it starts to slow. The windows are tinted so we can't see inside. We stay close to each other and the truck goes slowly to one side of us, then stops. The window begins to roll down on the driver's side. My eyes are focused on what is going to appear on the inside of this truck. The music is so loud and the window is going down intentionally slow. Then, two big eyes appear. The eyes have blue paint all around them and black eyeliner directly around the eye which makes the man's dark eyes look even more piercing. The window moves down a little further and exposes the huge red foam nose.

"Jesus." Kora says.

"Not exactly." The clown answers with no emotion.

"What do you want!" I scream at the clown.

It is the same clown from the circus tent. The corners of his mouth turn in an upward fashion to produce a very creepy smile as he looks directly at me. "Just imagine" He says. He then rolls the window back up, turns the vehicle around in the direction he had come and starts driving away slowly.

"Let's get the hell out of here." Isaac says.

Kora grabs the back of my arm and starts to move me forward. I look over at her and her face is stricken with fear. Everyone else bunches around us as we walk at a fast pace down the beach. The music is getting further away. My shoulders began to relax. As I look back to check the status of the truck I see that it is turning around, heading back toward us.

"Guys!" I yell and point at the truck at the same time.

"Shit!" Isaac yells. "Everybody run!"

I start running faster than I thought I was capable of. Not too far down the beach I see a huge green structure of some sort. I have an instant flashback of being here before. In this same spot… on this same beach. As we get close to the huge green thing, I notice that it is an island.

I look over my shoulder once more and the ice cream truck has sped up and is within feet of reaching us. We split into two groups, Isaac and kora go to the right and me, Jackson and Sophie to the left. The truck drives straight down the middle of us and continues until he is just about to the island then slams on the brakes. The truck skids out in the sand and ends up facing back toward us again. We have not stopped running. Jackson instructs us to keep going. I can see the water as we approach the embankment. It looks like a pretty strong current but none of us even hesitate. We jump in and the current grabs hold of us. It takes a little bit but we all end up safely on the embankment of the island.

After we catch our breath and crawl up out of the water, we walk away to look around. The island is thick with trees. I turn and look across the water and see the ice cream truck driving slowly away from the edge of the water. I plop down on the ground. "Let's just sit for another minute." I say.

"Good idea." Sophie agrees.

Jackson stays standing studying our surroundings. "Hey." He hollers, "There is some sort of tree fort in that tree."

"You should climb up and look around." I suggest with half a smile on my face.

He looks back at me and smiles, "Okay."

Jackson heads toward the tree he sees the structure in and Isaac jumps up to join him.

I watch as they walk together toward a huge tree that is surrounded by other huge trees. I can see there are steps on the front of this particular tree. They are made of wood and nailed to its large trunk, going all the way up to what must be the entrance of the fort. Jackson goes first and begins the climb, Isaac following right behind. The platform for the bottom of the fort is quite high up in the tree. They both enter the structure and disappear from site. After a few moments Isaac sticks his head out of the opening and yells, "This is so cool! We can see forever. And guess what I spy with my little eye?"

"Oh good Lord Isaac. What could it be?" Kora asks.

"A fair!" He yells back. I can see the rides, food booths, there are even pony rides for those interested!" He chuckles and ducks back in out of site.

"Seriously" Kora says as she stands up and heads toward the tree. "See any killer clowns?" She yells as she walks.

"Not yet." Isaac answers.

"A fair." Kora says as she continues walking. "That is where my mother's killer, my apparent father, said he worked. At a traveling fair. That was another reason he was absent...according to him. Thank God for that."

I lay my head back down and close my eyes. I guess we have become numb to the craziness of this place. The craziness of our pasts. How am I able to even crack a smile here, I wonder. I guess survival is an automatic response that we all have, the will to survive is the best tool we have.

To act in a somewhat normal manner while experiencing horrific events, one after another,

seems unrealistic and yet that is part of our survival strategy.

"Hey!" Kora is yelling from the same opening Isaac had been. "You have to check this out!"

I sit up and notice Sophie sitting by the edge of the water. I walk over and sit down next to her. "You ok?" I ask.

"None of this is ok Celeste. My god. I feel like I'm living inside my mother's head with her god damn insane visions!"

"Maybe your mother wasn't crazy after all."

Sophie looked directly at me, "She spent a huge portion of her life locked up and treated as a crazy person. But just maybe she wasn't? Well that's just a great thought."

"I just meant that nothing has made much sense for our whole life. But we are survivors." I tell her.

"For what? Why are we trying to survive so intently? What's it all for?"

"I think our automatic response to survive is something we don't control, it just happens naturally. Haven't you ever heard the saying God gives his toughest battles to his strongest soldiers. Or something like that" I ask.

"No. I haven't. And that doesn't make any sense. Or maybe it does. I don't know."

I decide to leave the conversation there for now and not comment any more.

We discuss heading to the fair. And of course decide to check it out. I guess we figure if it appears to us then it is something we are meant to check into. Being that we still have no answers to help us move on with our lives I figure everything is a possible clue to the puzzle. A puzzle with so many pieces that I have been trying to put together for quite a long time now and still so many openings and fragments that need to find their place scattered about.

As we near the first set of tents, the smell of deep fried everything floats in the air. The smells are wonderful. I realize that we have not eaten anything for quite some time.

"We should eat." I announce to the others.

"Smells that way." Sophie replies.

Isaac chimes in. "For some reason I don't feel hungry, I should be starving, but I will eat every smell out there. Smells soooo good."

"I can't remember the last time I was at a fair." Jackson shares.

I stop to look at everyone. "Just keep in mind that nothing here is truly pleasing. It seems as though it is going to be but then the cruel reality of this place hits us. Every time."

"That is all very true. And even though that is the case I think I am going to hunt down an elephant ear before the latter part of that statement begins." Isaac starts walking again toward the tents. "Besides, haven't we adjusted pretty well to suffering and discomfort?"

"Let's stay together as usual please." Jackson says as he runs past me to catch up with Isaac.

One thing that has remained the same is our personalities. Jackson, the responsible one. Always wanting to take care of everyone and everything. Isaac, puts on a brave face using humor to mask his pain. Kora, sweet and smart and at the same time defiant and strong. Cousin Sophie, Often the victim in need of rescue and yet her story is the most unclear. But also has a wisdom about her that surpasses her years in this world. Quiet and thoughtful always. And me, hard to identify oneself. I guess I feel like the therapist. Trying to help heal the heartbreaks.

As we approach the first tent there is a very tall man with his back turned to us. He is wearing a multi colored striped suit jacket. There are colors of light pinks, silvers and blues. We stand very still until the man turns and looks at us. He looks like a normal man in his early sixties. His smile is wide and he welcomes us to the state fair. Jackson asks what state. The man stares at Jackson with this confused look on his face. After a few more seconds he answers, "Why, I am not sure son. I would guess it is a very nice state though. Maybe the gentleman across the way might know. Perhaps you would like me to go over there and ask?"

Jackson is very polite but looks as concerned as I am feeling with the man's answer. "Oh no sir. Don't worry about it.

"I should know where I'm at." Jackson chuckles nervously.

"Folks! Folks!" The man across the way in another tent is yelling at us. We direct our attention his way. He is waving us to come over. This man is dressed very differently. He is wearing what looks like a light blue suit. The jacket is very dirty and has holes scattered in different areas as well. His pants are too short, going down to the ankles and he is wearing bright orange socks. There is a bright orange flower stuck behind his right ear. The man is short and plump and appears to be sweating. "Well come on." The man says to us. "Don't be shy. Step right up folks."

"What are we stepping up to?" I ask.

The man moves his eyes to meet mine. His smiles dissipates slowly and he gets the same confused look the man at the other tent had gotten. "Well," He pauses for a moment and looks up to the sky as if the answer might be there, "I'm not really sure now. Maybe I should check and I will be right back folks."

I, as Jackson had, stop the man and let him know that he did not need to do that. We will stop back later and he can check while we are gone. He excitedly agreed and we all send a smile his way as we walk away.

We continue walking in the center of the long row of tents. There are people yelling to us from each tent.

Some want us to come to their tent and others just seem to be repeating the same welcoming line over and over again. I move my gaze to investigate the person yelling as we walk by each and every one. They are all different and unique in nature. As we approach the end of the row of tents and near the food vendors the smells emitting becomes very strong. From deep fried foods to caramel smells to citrusy, sweet barbeque and so many other mouth-watering aromas. Isaac takes off running ahead. I smile to myself watching him. He looks like the boy I met back at the asylum. Excited and full of life. Jackson yells to him that we need to stay together. Isaac turns his head and has his usual big grinned smile, his blue eyes sparkle in the sun. "Get up here and get you some then!" Isaac yells to us.

We approach the booth where Isaac is standing and I notice a gentleman sitting on a small stool with his back to us. He is sitting in front of what appears to be some sort of fryer sitting on the ground. I watch as the man picks up a long hotdog from a cooler and places it on a stick, then dips the hotdog into what looks like a drink pitcher filled with batter. He then places it in the fryer. "Corndogs!" Sophie yells.

"Can we have five please." Kora says.

The short chubby lady with the round red cheeks smiles at us and nods. "Why of course you can."

She bent over and grabbed five pre wrapped corn dogs from under her wooden counter and set them down for us to grab. It dawns on me, we don't have any money. I mention this to the lady and she gets that same confused look on her. "Why I think that will be okay sweetheart."

My eyes scan the others and they look just as confused as I'm sure I do. We all grab a corndog, smile and thank the lady as we walk away. I unwrap the foil around my dog and take a bite. It practically melts in my mouth. I have never had anything so delicious! "Celeste?" Sophie's voice catches my attention. I look over and everyone is laughing.

"What are you doing to that corndog?" Jackson asks

"Enjoying it!" I say as I laugh.

As we stroll, we get snow cones, funnel cakes, french-fries and caramel apples. Oh and cotton candy. Did not have to pay for any of it. All of it tasted out of this world good.

When we get to the end of the food booths, I notice a wide open space all around. It looks like someone set this fair down in the middle of nowhere. I have no idea how much time we spent walking around the fair, time seems to be irrelevant here. I spin around another time to look at our surroundings and this time there are rides. Fair rides all around. "What in the hell." I say as I laugh out loud.

Isaac steps in front of me. "Not sure we should trust getting on any of those."

Everyone agrees with Isaac. As fun as they look, I'm sure something horrific could be waiting for us on any one of those rides.

We continue walking toward some of the rides, paying attention to our surroundings as we go. All of a sudden, I see a little girl walking in the same direction as us. She is a row over from us, kind of darting in and out of view, being obstructed by a ride here and there. That is the first person other than a worker we have seen. I let the others know, we all pay attention to where she is. A couple of us try to yell out to her but she doesn't stop. A few times she giggles and seems to run faster. Suddenly, Isaac gives chase. He is running towards the last spot we saw her. Jackson yells for him to stop. I yell that he is going to scare her. He slows his pace and turns toward us. He slumps over, winded, and puts his hands on his knees. "What are you doing?" Kora screams at him.

Isaac looks at her. "Trying to get answers Kora. That is the same little girl that was on the raft earlier."

We decide it's time to sit and figure out where to go next. The conversation is going well but then we hear a noise coming from behind the ferris wheel. It sounds like someone running and bumping into the long metal looking wall situated behind it. Jackson and Isaac get to their feet. Our eyes are all fixated on following the noise. Then it becomes apparent as to what is making the noise. Children! It looks like about five of them.

They are running and purposely letting themselves bounce off the metal as they go. They are all giggling and have big smiles. The little girl we saw earlier is in the group with these children. Jackson begins to open his mouth as though he is going to yell but Isaac stops him. Telling him it's no use. Kids can't help us anyway. What would they know? He said.

"What happened to getting answers Isaac? Those are the same kids. I would like to know why they keep showing up wherever we are?" Jackson says but doesn't really expect anyone to have an answer. Isaac just shrugs.

Isaac looks around, "I guess I change my mind on what I should do frequently, kind of like this place, changing frequently."

Everyone stands and we begin to head out of the fair perimeter. We are going to venture beyond this section of wherever we are. We are just a short way outside of the fairgrounds and suddenly hear crying. It sounds like children crying, then one of them screaming. "What the hell!" Jackson hollers.

"I think we should ignore it." I say. "Just have a bad feeling about investigating that."

"I think we should listen to Celeste." Kora says.

You could hear a pin drop. Everyone is standing still and quiet listening for more crying, screaming or any other noise. We hear nothing.

The sky is a beautiful blue color with white puffy clouds. The air is warm with a nice breeze. We begin to walk toward the nothingness that lies ahead. I notice as we walk a bit further there seems to be a community of houses in the direction we are heading. It seems like an endless line of homes...more like shacks going in each direction. None of the others mention the houses or that they see them until we get a bit closer. I notice the houses all appear to be in ruins. There is no road running down what seems to be the middle of this community, just a dirt path wide enough for a vehicle if need be. I look at the others and can tell by the expressions on their faces that they are as apprehensive as I feel heading toward this dilapidated looking town. As we get closer yet it appears to have swamps all around. We all look toward Jackson who by the look on his face has noticed this as well.

As usual we proceed, with caution, but nevertheless proceed. We reach the beaten up dirt path that enters the territory. I look over at Kora because suddenly I feel a slight vibration under my feet. She is looking at the ground so I assume she feels it as well. Jackson who is a few steps in front of me turns slowly and looks directly behind me. "What?" I ask.

"You can't hear that?" He answers without looking at me.

Before I have a chance to answer I hear a low rumbling noise. Everyone is looking in the same direction as Jackson at this point. The rumbling is getting louder. "Come on." Jackson says.

We follow him toward one of the structures that is close to us. Jackson kicks the front door open. The condition inside the abandoned house is just as bad if not worse than the outside. There is an awful pungent smell. I put my hand up to my nose and try to breathe only through my mouth. We follow Jackson up the crooked stairs to the second floor. The smell is not quite as strong. I notice some windows either broken or opened up and fresh air is blowing in throughout some of the rooms. I follow everyone into a room that is facing the way we heard the noise coming from. The rumbling is very loud now, we can hear it through the walls and there is a huge cloud of dust emitting from the ground flowing high into the sky. Suddenly there is a loud screeching sound. I squint to try and see what is heading our way until I can make it out. They are horses! Horses with riders. I take a step back from the window. The riders have the shape of a man but the form is not skin, instead it looks like a dark mist making the outline of a man. As the horse gallops toward us I can make out a skeletal looking face with very thin skin covering parts of it. The hands holding the reins looked the same. Without warning, a strong wind starts blowing into the room. Then an inhuman sounding scream. I put my hands up to my ears to block the horrible sound.

I hear a crackling sound and realize it is coming from the window. Jackson hollers for everyone to get down. I barely get to my knees and the window shatters. Glass sprays everywhere.

The wind comes howling into the room. Isaac is lying next to me on the floor and I can see Kora across the room crouched by what I assume is a closet door with her head in her knees. Sophie's knee jabs me in the back as she moves. I can't see where Jackson is. I sit still and listen. Everything has become eerily quiet. "Nobody move yet." It's Jackson. He was behind Sophie.

Then, there is a creaking noise coming from downstairs. It sounds like someone is walking. Whatever it is weighs heavy on the rickety floors. Seconds later, it becomes obvious that the footsteps are ascending up the stairs. Nobody is moving. I am watching the door to the room we are in. Jackson had closed it once we were inside. The knob on the door begins to turn slowly. Then the door itself begins to gradually open. Once it becomes completely open I cannot see anything, there is nothing there. I can see Isaac shift out of my peripheral vision. His eyes are locked into something. I follow his gaze out into the hallway and see a long, skinny skeletal hand starting its entrance into the room. The fingers are crawling up the door frame.

There is only a small part of the bony arm visible at this point extended from the hallway. Then something enters, a young man stands by the door. He is covered in blood and has only one arm. The other is barely attached and without a choice dangles at his side. His skin is a shade of gray but also blackened in some areas of it. His eyes are vacant, like no one is in there. Jackson stands up, "Toby?" Without warning, the awful screaming starts up again.

Everything goes black...

The Hunt

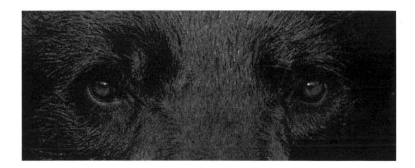

I feel a warm breeze blowing on my face. I struggle to open my eyes. What feels like a wet tongue begins licking at my right ear. This jolts me up. I am face to face with the most adorable bunny. It is brown in color and sitting on its hind legs. This little bunny is staring right into my eyes. Then it begins thumping. "What are you doing?" I ask, fully expecting it possible for this animal to answer me. It doesn't move but begins whimpering. I put my hand up to pet its head when suddenly a loud noise startles the little thing and it hops away quickly. It sounded like a gunshot but I couldn't be sure.

"What was that?" Kora asks.

I turn to see if we are all still together. Kora is the only one I see. "Where are the others? I ask.

"I don't know. I just woke up."

Just then Isaac and Jackson come walking out of the woods that surround the entire area I can see.

Jackson runs toward us, "Where is Sophie?"

"We just woke up." I tell him.

He looks around in all directions and then begins yelling for her. There is a sweet smell in the air. The wind blows softly. I stand up to help Jackson find Sophie. Kora joins us and Isaac is already ahead walking the edge of the woodland searching. Before long Isaac notices her lying just off the trail in a clearing. Jackson is the first to reach her. He starts to shake her lightly. She forms a smile on her face before opening her eyes. "I know that shake." She says. Jackson exhales loudly and sits back with the look of relief on his face.

We all take in our new surroundings. The clearing we found Sophie in has just a few trees and very tall grass. I feel it was lucky Isaac noticed her as I look around again and realize how easy it would be to disappear in what looks like a vast meadow. The sweet smell appears to be coming from all the wild honeysuckle that blankets the entire clearing we are in. Hummingbirds are everywhere, flying from one flower to the next. I focus in on one of the little birds hovering in air as its long bill inserts in and out of the pretty white petals. Koras voice brings me out of my daze. "You ready to move on?" She is asking.

I look toward her voice and see that she has her hand extended out to me. I take her hand in mine and we start walking across the open grassland heading toward the tree line at the other end. The hummingbirds continue their activity as we pass by, hovering next to the flower they had chosen.

We are almost to the end of the spacious meadow when Sophie spots what looks like a covered bridge straight ahead. It looks old and frayed. It at one time I can tell was red in color. When we get close, we hear children's voices. It sounds like they are playing. We hear laughter and other noises coming from somewhere under the bridge. "Hello?" Kora yells. The noises stop. Again Kora yells, "Hello!" No response. Then, a little boy appears at the top of hill by the edge of the bridge.

Isaac takes a step toward him and smiles. "Hi. My name is Isaac. Who are you?"

The boy smiles back. Then he turns and darts back down the hill. Isaac takes chase after him, the rest of us follow. By the time we get to the bottom of the hill the children are all running away. It looks like there are about five of them. The same group of kids! The boy looks like he is around ten years old. Isaac is continuing the chase so Jackson yells for him to stop. "Why are we chasing these kids again Isaac?" Isaac begins to laugh, shakes his head in a way that we take as, I have no idea. We climb back up the hill and decide to cross the bridge and continue heading in the same direction.

The bridge is fairly long and once we get to the other side I instantly feel the change in the air. It is also evident immediately that it is snowing. Is this the threshold to winter I wonder. It looks like we are in a snow globe the way the snow is falling in a slow motion fashion. The trees and ground are covered in snow and everything is glistening, giving the appearance of sparkling diamonds everywhere. It really is beautiful. And the light is able to shine through, the tree lines seem to widen and not be as thick in this spot. Kora falls into the snow and makes a snow angel. I do the same. A short snowball fight happens, then we realize once again where we are and stop almost immediately. "I'm not even cold." Kora says.

"Me either." I add. "It's weird, I felt the temperature change when we first stepped off the bridge. This place is so mysterious, to say the least."

"No shit!" Jackson acknowledges. "Should we proceed forward or go back across the bridge? What do you guys think?"

"Let's move on. Keep moving forward." I said.

Just then, there is a crunching noise coming from the hill, from the same side of the bridge we are. I think it must be the kids again. They are probably following us. "Come on out guys." Sophie yells. "You don't have to be afraid. We aren't going to hurt you." She adds. The brush next to the bridge begins to move. We stand still, patiently waiting for the children to come out.

The first thing I notice is fur, brown fur. It appears through a section in the brush. I follow the fur with my eyes and notice there are claws, long sharp claws attached to a huge foot. I look around at everyone and can tell by the looks on their faces they notice the same thing. "RUN!" Jackson shouts. Everyone takes off running, we are following Jackson. Sophie is in front of me and I accidentally step on the back of her shoe which makes her trip and fall. I instantly stop and turn around to help her up. As I grab hold of her arm to pull her to her feet, I look up to see a monster of a bear running right toward us! As its two front feet hit the ground, all of the fat and muscle on its entire body rolls. Sophie is trying to stand faster than her feet want to work and she falls back again. My heart is beating heavy in my ears, it feels like they are going to explode. "Let's go!" I scream. We are up and running again but the bear has gained so much ground and was now so close I can hear its deep breathing. It is making this horrifying grunting noise and its breaths are very heavy. My thought is to stop running and face it. We are not going to be able to outrun this thing. It has basically caught up to us in a matter of seconds.

"Stop!" I scream as I turn my body around and face the bear. It is right there, easily within a few steps from catching anyone of us! Everyone turns around and also stop. We begin to scream at the bear, who also stops running. The giant beast takes a couple steps back.

It is roaring loudly back at us and digging into the dirt with one of its large paws. It takes a couple steps toward us and we take a couple steps back at the same time. The bear continues walking toward us and we continue taking steps back.

I am so focused on this bear, I am not taking my eyes off of it. Suddenly, my foot comes out from underneath me and I land on my stomach with my face in the ground. I begin sliding backwards down a hill. I look to my left and see Jackson and Sophie sliding a bit ahead of me. I pick my head up to look back toward the top of the hill and Kora is sliding fast, right at my face, and Isaac is to the right of us. I am trying to move over so Kora doesn't run into me, but instead of moving over my foot catches and I begin rolling down the hill which is made up of little black pebbles. My head hits the ground hard at the bottom and I stop instantly. I land with my head facing the hill we just slid down. It takes me a moment to get my bearings but manage to pick my head up and look up the hill, I can see the bear sliding down, trying to get control of its heavy body. It is sliding face first and putting its front legs in front of its massive body in a laying position to try and slow down. "We are going to die." I say.

"No, we are not!" Isaac yells back. "Get up! Everyone up, let's go!" He grabs a large stick from the ground and we start to run again. Kora notices a trail and hollers for everyone to go that way, which we do.

I cannot hear the bear yet, I look behind as I am running and don't see it, but we have went around many sharp corners. As we round the next corner there is a cabin in site, not too far down the trail. Everyone sees it and begins running for it. Jackson gets there first and kicks the door open with great force. He holds it open as we all run inside and then slams it shut. I collapse on the floor, as Jackson and Isaac shove the table from the middle of the room tight up against the door. Kora plants her face to the window that is right next to the door.

"I don't see it!" Kora says breathlessly

"Stay there and keep a look out." Jackson tells her. "I am going to make sure there is no other way in here. Holler if you see it coming."

Kora does as Jackson instructs. I am still trying to catch my breath lying on the floor. Sophie plops on the couch and is now sobbing. Isaac is staring out the window on the other side of the door, still holding the large stick in his hand which is visibly quivering. I get up and walk over to Isaac and place my hand on his to help steady the stick from shaking. "It's coming." Kora said in a whisper.

"No!" Sophie yelled as she sat up.

Jackson comes back into the room and runs to the window, "Shit," he said. We all gather in front of the window and watch the bear walk slowly toward the cabin. As it gets closer, it starts transforming.

The face and neck become human like, then the arms and legs. Finally, it is no longer a bear. It is a man.

It is my grandfather! He stops once he is close to the front door. Everyone is standing still with mouths open in disbelief of what we are witnessing. I open the front door without thinking.

"Hello Celeste." Grandfather says. "I don't have much time but I need to tell you that you are not here for me. I am here of my own accord and must suffer through and find my own redemption.

"You're a bear?" I asked with tears in my eyes.

"I am many things, but what I really am, is hunted. This is a place for me to realize my worst sins. Nothing you do here will change that or make the process move any faster for me."

"I don't understand. That is why I came... for you."

Just then we hear what sounds like gunshots. Isaac grabs me from behind, drags me back inside and slams the door shut. We both fall to the floor, everyone else drops to the floor as well. I pull myself up to the window sill to look out and see a white tail deer running back into the woods. Then, out of the trail that we were on, comes two men with rifles in hand. They are on foot but running at a speed that would be impossible for a human to achieve. They are chasing the deer... who is probably not really a deer, but my grandfather!

"What did he mean?" I ask. Everyone shakes their head to let me know that they are just as puzzled by what happened, what was said, the fact that a killer bear just transformed into my grandfather and then into a deer. Every new bizarre event seems to outdo the one prior. I think I am still trying to cling to some sort of normalcy where there isn't any left.

We have been sitting in silence for quite some time when a noise comes from the back of the cabin. "What is that?" I turn in the direction the noise came from.

"It sounds like giggling." Kora says.

"There it is again!" Sophie yells.

I begin to walk toward the noise. Kora follows right beside me. There is a small window in the very back area of the cabin. The window is open, the noise is coming from outside. We both hurry to the window and look out. "It's those children again!" I exclaim.

"Where are they?" Isaac asks as he runs to the window to get a look. The children are playing what looks like ring around the rosy. They all have creepy looking masks on. The masks look to be made of brown paper bags with glued on strings of yarn for hair and small holes cut out for their eyes. It looks as though they used color crayons to decorate the face area in a clown like fashion.

"What are they?" Isaac says out loud. "Let's go see if they will talk to us. They must want to or they wouldn't keep showing up" He says.

As we walk out the front door and head toward the back we can still hear the singing. 'Ring around the Rosie, pockets full of posies, ashes, ashes.' And then they squeal and giggle as they fall to the ground. The biggest boy notices us first. He stands up and points at us. All of the other children turn their attention to us. These kids are so intense, kind of eerie, especially with those homemade masks on. "Hi." Sophie says in her sweetest voice. All of the children giggle, take their masks off, let them fall to the ground and smile at us. Then one at a time they begin mocking Sophie, each one saying hi over and over again.

"Stop it!" Jackson hollers at them. "Who in the hell are you kids?"

The littlest one steps forward and smiles big, "We are the Changelings." She turns around, I notice that the back of her dress was quite dirty on the bottom from the ground. The biggest boy comes and takes her hand and they begin to walk toward the woods behind the cabin. The other three children follow. The little girl looks over her shoulder and gave us another big smile as she walks away.

None of us try to follow or stop them. "Weird ass kids." Kora says.

"Hey." Sophie interjects.

Kora continues. "I'm sorry. They make me uncomfortable. It seems like they are intentionally trying to."

"Yeah, I get it. I'm just trying not to freak out about the kids when there are so many other things to be concerned about." Sophie explains.

"We are all freaked out here guys, ok. Let's try and stay as calm as reasonably possible." I say.

The wind picks up and begins to blow really hard. "We better get back in the cabin until we figure out what to do next." Jackson suggests.

"Yes." Sophie agrees.

We follow Isaac heading back to the front of the cabin. The wind starts blowing even harder. I look up at the tree tops and they are bent over following the direction of the wind. In the short time it takes us to get back in the cabin, the wind is blowing so hard it is difficult to shut the door. Once inside, as I look around the room, what once was the 'Fab Five', no longer looks like the people I knew. Our confidence is fading and we are beginning to look defeated. I wonder how this is going to turn out if things continue the way they have so far. We were so certain of what our mission was when we choose to climb those slides, now it seems as though we may have been wrong about that. I sit down in a chair by one of the windows looking out at the place we ended up in. After a few minutes of gazing out the window, I close my eyes and try to make sense of what is happening and what we are supposed to do. I allow myself to slip into a deep meditative state, slowing my breathing and letting my body become more limp and relaxed. A whistling sound enters my mind.

It is a familiar tune and is getting louder. Suddenly, I am startled out of my dream like state when I hear Sophie say, "Now what."

My eyes pop open, Jackson and Sophie are standing next to me peering out the window. I focus my eyes on where they are looking. A very tall, thin man is walking toward the cabin. He is well dressed in what appears to be a suit and tie. As he gets closer I can see that he is the one whistling. The tune is familiar and ominous. All five of us are at the window watching this man approach, he has his hands clasped behind his back and walks with a purpose. His head is held high and he continues whistling even after he focuses on us. "All around the mulberry bush, the monkey chased the weasel." Isaac sings.

"Oh yes, I knew I knew that song." I say.

Now the man has reached the window. The wind that was ready to blow the cabin away, stops abruptly. The window is open so the man comes right up to it and rests his hands on the sill. He stops whistling and looks right at Isaac and sings, "The monkey stopped to pull up his sock, Pop! Goes the weasel."

"Who are you?" Isaac asks.

"I know you." I interrupt the man from answering. "Well, I don't know you but I have seen you before."

"Oh?" The man turns his attention to me.

"I think. It was a long time ago. At my grandfather's camp. I, I had gotten lost, in the woods, and I saw you."

"Where was that my dear?" He raised one eyebrow when he asked.

"Near Pentington, Michigan. I grew up in Pentington. My grandfather's camp isn't, wasn't too far from there."

"Never been there." The man said very matter of fact.

I am studying his face and even though he comes across as being quite old, he doesn't have hardly any wrinkles. His face is so thin it looks caved in in it's appearance, this exaggerated his mouth and made it look oversized. His eyes are so dark, they look black. And he is balding but has some thin hair around the side of his head and a few strands across the top.

"Of course, at my age," The man says. "Maybe there are places one has been but has lost memory of. Who's to say for sure. I have been many places. Anyway, I am looking for my children. Have you seen them?"

"Children?" I say

The man stands up straight and takes in a deep breath of air, exhaling loudly. "I have five children running around here. They are so playful and so very good at hiding. They find it funny to watch me search. Sometime as I am walking, I hear their laughter. I just smile and continue calling their names. I suppose it is a game we play. Have been playing for a long time and somehow they never tire of it. And I never quit." A smile comes across his face so big it exaggerates his mouth even more.

"We have seen children several times." I say. "They never let us get close. We have tried to approach and talk to them but they ran off every time. I don't know if those were your children, they are quite young."

The man squints his eyes and looks at everyone before returning his gaze to me. "I'm not sure how old my children are now. How does one measure? Besides it seems my search is over and the game has come to an end. I wasn't sure this day would ever come." Then he takes a step back from the window. He begins to look each of us over, taking the time to study us at length. As he inhales loudly he raises his head up toward the sky, then lowers it down looking our way again. He has a stern look on his face when in a low but clear voice he says, "Hello my children."

And then…everything went black.

Redemption

The two brothers sat in the living room of the old lighthouse they called home. Their parent's had owned this beautiful place and their father's parents before them. In fact, Jim and Dan's family had owned this lighthouse as far back as records go.

There was a lot of work to keep an old structure like this going and making sure it was able to perform the service it was intended to when it was built.

The lighthouse let the passing ships know where they were, and where they were was one of the most dangerous spots in Lake Superior. Deceiving shore lines that were lined with tall cliffs led boats to believe the depth of the water to be greater than it was. Rock piles lined this area that lay hidden just under the surface which kept the captains of the boats alert at all times when passing through. Huge swells were always present due to the fact that the water shallows significantly and the winds seemed to whip in all directions like a constant tornado churning up the water. There have been many ships that have gone down right in front of the colossal lighthouse in what has become known as the shipwreck graveyard.

The alarm was very loud. Loud enough to wake a person up out of the dead of sleep. The sound was unmistakable. It didn't go off every day, not even necessarily every week, in fact it barely sounded at all. But when it did Jim and Dan jumped to attention. They had to move fast, and that's exactly what they did on this night. It must have been just past 8:00 P.M. It was summer so it was still light out. The two moved quickly into the shed out behind the house to put their slickers on and proceeded to head to the dock where their boat was. The cliff that they needed to get to via water was not far.

The problem wasn't the distance, but always the condition of the great lake. It took some experienced driving to maneuver around in the giant waves. They did have a spotlight on the front of the boat but they would not need it tonight, there should be plenty of daylight left. As they rounded the corner and went past the beautiful water caves they could see all five bodies floating face down. The rescue boat was having a difficult time getting to them. Meanwhile, each body continued to rise and fall in the huge swells that Lake Superior had been producing all day. "Those poor people. Christ." Dan said.

"Wonder if they found anything." Jim thought out loud.

Dan gave him an angry look. "Don't start your rambling about that damn island Jim. The only thing these young people found was a tall cliff and a long drop into a deep water."

Dan and Jim both looked upward to the top of the cliff that stood high above their boat in the water. "Well, we know what we have to do, and that's what needs to get done right now. Get these bodies out of the water and get them to Mr. Meta before anyone else sees them. Same as all the rest. "Jim stated nervously.

New Beginnings

I wake in a new place. We are no longer in the cabin. It looks like we are on a beach, a different beach from before, all of us are still together.

The sand is the color of snow and the water again is the color of the most perfect turquoise gem. The lake didn't have so much as a ripple of water moving about. The winged man's reflection in the water is a perfect mirrored image of his flight. I am mesmerized to say the least, along with everyone else.

We are standing shoulder to shoulder in a line watching this thing circling, getting closer to the ground with each pass. Finally it begins its descent.

This living thing lands not too far away from us. Initially, it keeps its knees bent so that it is almost touching the ground and has his head lowered facing the ground. I anxiously watch as he begins to straighten and stand. He is huge and appears to have the face and body of a man. He must stand at least seven feet tall. The arms and legs bulge with muscle, the neck is almost as thick as his shoulders and has a bald head with a very strong looking, chiseled face. He stands tall and is looking in our direction, his eyes are scanning each of us. I notice at that point that he has quite a lot of scars, there are some on every visible part of his body that is showing from out of the cloth like clothing he has on.

He takes a step toward us and speaks. "I am Ramiel. I am here to help you finish your journey successfully."

Nobody answers or says anything for at least a minute. Including Ramiel.

"What journey?' Isaac finally breaks the silence with.

"You have entered Gehenna, as you know. Intentionally and with permission from the watchers."

"What are you?" Sophia asked

"I am a son of God."

Then, a noise comes from behind him. I am in awe as he extends his wings. They must be eight feet across with layers of black feathers. He watches our reactions and then closes them.

I can still see some of the wings coming up from behind his shoulders when they are not open. "I have been waiting for the right time to make contact with all of you. I had to be certain that I understood the vision I had."

I was afraid to ask but did anyway, "What vision?"

"You will all be given another chance. You see, what really defines us is how well we rise after falling."

"Good." Jackson stated. "I am more than ready to go home."

Ramiel looked at Jackson with what appeared to be sympathetic eyes. "You all have lost your previous life form when you hit the waters of Lake Superior. Those bodies have been retrieved from that water. They were brought to another fallen angel, his name is Metatron. We must keep Gehenna alive for those who need penance from the life they are living or those such as yourselves who will not understand their true life lesson. Those like you who have ventured off your intended path so far that intervention was necessary.

"Our path was laid out for us. I certainly didn't choose it." Sophie interjects.

The fallen angel looks at Sophie and then to all of us and in a very loud voice that seemed to be demanding attention said, "FORGIVENESS. Your purpose was to learn, understand, have the ability to and teach the knowledge of forgiving." Ramiel looks toward Jackson, "Including ones-self. You all had much to work with. Instead, it was teaching you other things...anger, resentment, selfishness, self loathing.

It may not have been worn on the surface but you held it within. None of these things needed to be discovered. The devil plants those in you at a very young age. You are not here to help or save anyone but yourselves. You have been reminded of certain things that needed to be forgiven but you had not been able to. It imprisons the one seeking forgiveness and the one choosing not to give it. You are among ones we have chosen. You will not be returning to what you have known, that is not even possible. You will be offered a new beginning."

Kora takes a few steps backward and has a look on her face as though she was going to run, it was a look of fear. It reminded me of being young and scared and not wanting to hear what someone was telling you because if you don't hear it, it means it isn't real. Her behaving like that set off a panic feeling in me.

"We are dead?" Kora asks softly.

"You are no longer from where you came." The fallen angel answers.

Ramiel notices the distressed look on most of our faces, he asks us all to sit so he can explain. He begins talking with a tone that is so calming, I find myself getting fixated on his voice and notice my anxiety is dissipating quickly.

"I have been here for a very long time. I have been watching all of you for a period of that time. It is what I do.

I have intervened with all of you at some point in your previous life because that is what I was told to do.

At times there was evidence of my presence so that when this day came you could remember. So that maybe it would help you understand and help with the doubt you all have with what I am telling you now." He then looked directly at me, "One of you have entered Gehenna before. You knew and felt as though you had entered another realm, but you couldn't stay. I brought you back to where you had come from. You weren't meant to be here then. You saw the town you will know, the structure you will call home and you also saw a man you will know. Gehenna can show you any surrounding it chooses and it can change in a flash. It can make you feel hot or cold, hungry or not, fearful or peaceful. It can present as the most stunningly beautiful place or as an absolutely spine-chilling dwelling. The myth people speak of is far from truth. The slides for instance signify the seven terraces of purgatory. The slides have become enveloped with these sins. One slide represents two of the deadly sins; greed and gluttony. They like to work together. Wanting to and doing to the extreme in regards to wealth and materialism. Another slide represents pride and sloth. Being so engrossed in one's self and their accomplishments it blinds them from the grace of our God and the other being so unaccomplished and idol they can't recognize that either. Then there is yet another slide signifying envy and lust. The desire for others situations or desires for personal pleasures. And finally we have our fourth slide that is wrapped in wrath. Fury instead of love and kindness. It makes no difference which slide you climb. It is merely the climb to your own personal purgatory enveloped with all of these great sins. The slides are connected through parallel and perpendicular lines. Dante's climb up the mountain was very difficult as was yours up the slides. When people who have an ability to 'travel' into other dimensions have been able to get a glimpse, they don't fully see Gehenna for what it truly is, they are not allowed to. They take what they are able to see and form a story to tell. This story is important in keeping the reality of Gehenna alive."

He continued moving his gaze amongst us all. "There are many of us that watch. I have fallen. I no longer get to be in the same place with my father. You see, some of us fallen angels are now in purgatory under the direction of the father, working on our own redemption. Where you are now is not the parallel world you have heard about growing up. This place you are in, known as Gehenna, is the place you end up when your induction is in limbo. You end up here awaiting a decision of where you get to go next. The myth has confused and mixed two true places into one. None of you get to go "home" yet. I am speaking of where you originated from. The place where we all originated from...In this new place, you will have a second chance to live your life like your father wants you to live it. You need to realize who your one true God is, you must worship only him in your next life and discover what you are there to learn, your purpose.

Only then will that emptiness in you be filled. Not everyone is awarded this opportunity, some stay here, in limbo for eternity. The fact that you all showed complete selflessness and have all suffered greatly is what has gotten you the reward of a second chance. Nothing from the past will carry with you to this new start. Your memories will be lost in transport to your new temporary home. You will have a fresh start, a clean slate and begin anew. You will feel pain again. It is going to be what you do to deal with your new sufferings that will help you get back to your real home. Then hopefully when your time ends this time we will not have to meet again. I hope that all of you will be able to go home at the end of this new journey. I will be watching as I have been as you begin this transition ...known as... "The Changelings".

I could hear Kora screaming the word no over and over again, and then... everything went black.